# THE ERIS RIDGE TRAIL

## LARRY HINKLE

# PRAISE FOR THE ERIS RIDGE TRAIL

"Larry Hinkle takes his readers on a labyrinthian cosmic walkabout where nothing is solid underfoot and absolutely nothing is safe. Fair warning: the narrative switchbacks along *The Eris Ridge Trail* are razor sharp and utterly mind-bending, so pack a compass before diving in, because you may never escape its pages."

— Clay McLeod Chapman, author of *Wake Up and Open Your Eyes*

"Hinkle doesn't just twist reality in his newest scarefest, he obliterates it, tossing his characters (and readers) into a supernatural blender that will take them through a maze of crashing dimensions filled with enough monsters and madness to tear his fictional world—and the minds of those lost within—to bloody ribbons. Enter at your own risk!"

— Philip Fracassi, author of *Boys in the Valley*

"*The Eris Ridge Trail* is a gripping story of survival, friendship, and hope reminiscent of a trip to King's Dark Tower."

— Tom Deady, Bram Stoker Award-winning author of *Haven*, *Eternal Darkness*, and *Stingy Jack*

"An unpredictable and thrilling expedition through an unreliable setting, *The Eris Ridge Trail* dishes out adventure, horror, romance, and a memorable cast of characters—both human and canine. Hinkle plays a game of reality hopscotch that will suck you in and keep you jumping until the very last page."

— James Chambers, Bram Stoker Award-winning author of *A Bright and Beautiful Eternal World* and *On the Night Border*

"With *The Eris Ridge Trail*, Larry Hinkle doesn't just reimagine the limits of horror and memory, friendship and grief, he explodes them. The stakes are treacherous, the settings full of peril, and the creatures are many-teethed. For those who dare to read before bed, consider yourselves warned: the monsters that follow you into sleep don't play by the normal rules of nightmares."

— Christa Carmen, Bram Stoker Award-winning and Shirley Jackson Award-nominated author of *The Daughters of Block Island*

"*The Eris Ridge Trail* has no damn right to contain as much as it does. It's a story that begins with a sinister maze, then portal-shunts into a labyrinth of badly behaved realities, traversed by well-behaved dogs and their reluctant humans. There are monsters and mysteries, and stars that shine darker than their alien skies. Hinkle has performed some mad origami of the imagination, and I am here for every fold and tuck."

— Neil McRobert, Talking Scared podcast

"Hinkle does a masterful job of keeping you at the edge of your seat, making you smile, and bringing you tears, while at the same time creating a whole new take on cosmic horror. It's a definite must-read!"

—JG Faherty, author of *Sins of the Father*, *The Nightmare Man*, and *Ragman*

"*The Eris Ridge Trail* is a haunting, unsettling, moving story —and not without hope. It's *The Ritual* meets *The Hunger* with a dash of *Mongrels*. A wild ride."

— Richard Thomas, Bram Stoker, Shirley Jackson, and Thriller Award finalist

"Hinkle's creative brilliance shines throughout a dangerous and mysterious world where no detail has gone unimagined. Filled with dread and suspense, his characters face their fate with visceral realism. Reminiscent of King's "In the Tall Grass" and "The Dark Tower" series, my only criticism is that *The Eris Ridge Trail* ends way too soon."

— EV Knight, Bram Stoker Award-winning author of *The Fourth Whore*

"*The Eris Ridge Trail* is another outstanding work of weird, dark fiction by Larry Hinkle, that leaves readers with but one trouble: no matter how much of Larry you read, you're left still wishing for more!"

— Eric J. Guignard, multiple award-winning author of *That Which Grows Wild* and *Doorways to the Deadeye*

"A mismatched group journey through a mind-bending maze of cosmic terror in this quirky tale of grief and isolation. Monstrous, off-kilter, and disorienting, Larry Hinkle's *The Eris Ridge Trail* is a chilling metaphor for our times."

— Lee Murray, five-time Bram Stoker Awards®-winning author of *Grotesque: Monster Stories*

"Hinkle has once again proven his worth as an up-and-coming author. *The Eris Ridge Trail* is a boldly creative journey into the cosmic realms, reminiscent of Dean

Koontz's writings, hyper-intelligent doggies and all. I loved every word."

— Bridgett Nelson, Splatterpunk Award-winning author of *Red Inside* and *A Bouquet of Viscera*

"What she said."

— Jeff Strand, Bram Stoker Award-winning author of *Snuggling the Grotesque*

The Eris Ridge Trail

Copyright © 2025 by Larry Hinkle

IngramSpark Paperback edition ISBN: 979-8-9924542-0-8

Published by Four Winds Bar Publishing

www.fourwindsbarpublishing.com

First edition: March 2025

Edited by Linda Nagle

Cover design by François Vaillancourt, www.francois-art.com

 Created with Vellum

*For Sammie and Koko (and Alli, Beavis, and Edna)*
*See ya on the other side*

# CHAPTER ONE

S helly Perkins' interview had lasted longer than she'd anticipated, so her watch read 9:00 when she pulled out of the parking lot of Old Bob's Corn Maize Spooktacular. Stars twinkled overhead, and the moon hung low on the horizon. She looked both ways, more out of habit than necessity this far out in the country, then turned left onto the empty two-lane road.

She'd joked earlier in the evening that her editor's directions were crap, and Old Bob's shortcut—he'd given her directions at the end of their interview—promised to take thirty minutes off her drive home. What was it he'd said? *The Eris Ridge Trail can get a bit hinky after dark, but with that car and tonight's full moon, you should be safe.*

The car in question was a 1978 Subaru wagon with four-wheel drive. Her father had bought the first one to hit the showroom floor as her graduation gift the previous spring. He'd been worried about her driving out here during the winter. Her job as a local reporter for the county paper—which she'd accepted before she'd even received her diploma—had been a bit boring up to this point, but she was sure her story on Old Bob's corn maze—sorry, *Corn Maize Spooktacular!*—had the potential to land her on the front page for the first time. Ironic, since Old Bob had told her that profiling his attraction was a busy-work story the editor gave to all new reporters.

But she and Old Bob—she still couldn't bring herself to think of him as just Bob—had hit it off right away; so well, in fact, that he'd shared some information with her he'd never told the other reporters.

Everyone knew about the disappearances at the maze over the years. She'd read the articles and the police reports when preparing her questions. The first was the original Old Bob, his grandfather. He'd walked into the corn one autumn night and had never come out. Bob's father, the second Old Bob, had seen it happen. The glow from his flashlight had faded away as if the batteries had died there and then. The police said his boot prints had gotten lighter and then stopped.

There were two other disappearances worth noting. A teenager named Joey Ramsey had snuck into the maze late one night with some friends to drink beer. The other boys said Joey had walked down another row to take a leak and hadn't come back. The police had written him off as a runaway, considering his father had a well-earned reputation as the town drunk. Nobody would've blamed Joey if he had left town.

The next disappearance, though, was harder to explain. A girl named Lisa Ranalli was walking the maze with some girlfriends on a busy Friday night in October. They reported that Lisa had stopped to tie her shoe. When a few minutes passed and she hadn't caught back up with them, they backtracked to look for her. But Lisa was gone.

Of course, there were lots of local legends about the

place, too. Strange lights, whispers in the corn, other noises. A couple even reported seeing a "crack in the sky" above the maze one night. These anecdotes would add a little color to her story, sure, but the new information was the real scoop. According to Old Bob, people had actually *appeared* in the maze.

Shelly pushed the cassette from her interview into the tape player on her stereo. The playback of their conversation filled the car's interior.

*"What do you mean, appearances?"*

*"I mean people who came out of the maze who never went in. We call 'em visitors."*

*"Wait, how do you know they'd never entered?"*

*"Security cameras. We had to put 'em up in '74, after the Ranalli girl disappeared. Only way we could keep our insurance. Got one at every corner of the maze, at the entrance and exit, and in the middle clearing where the scarecrow hangs. We also keep a strict headcount matched against ticket sales. Nobody can get in or out of the maze without us knowing about it."*

*"But you're saying someone did. How many times did this happen?"*

*"My dad said it happened to him once, but he didn't like to talk about it. I could tell it really bothered him."*

*"What about you? Did you ever see any of these visitors?"*

*"Once. Couple of kids stumbled out of the maze one afternoon. One of 'em said some bullies had chased them into it the day before."*

*"But the cameras didn't pick them up, going in?"*

*"Nope. And they were on during the day that week cuz we had a big crew finishing up the harvest. Lotta temporary help running around who I didn't know, so I needed to keep an eye on 'em. Between the cameras and that many folks choring, no way those kids coulda snuck in during the day. We leave the cameras*

*on at night, too, and do a sweep when we shut it down and another when we start work the next morning. There's no record of those boys going in. He could have been lying, but..."*

"But you sound like you believe him."

"I don't know. If he was lying, kid was a damn good actor. *Never saw anyone as scared as he was. Told me they'd been in there overnight. In fact, he said it was still night in there when they'd crashed through that last row into the parking lot. Talked about seeing two moons in the sky, and how the stars and constellations were all wrong. Said there was a giant beast with orange eyes stalking the rows, and that one of the bullies peeled his own face off.*"

Shelly shuddered and ejected the tape. A road sign indicated the Eris Ridge Trail was just ahead. Turning off the main road, she considered her options. In her headlights, the trail appeared to be hard-packed gravel. Old Bob had said the county was technically in charge of it, but since it ran flat the whole way, they graded it only twice a year and left the routine maintenance up to the locals. There were no streetlights, but the full moon provided plenty of illumination. Shelly hesitated, but decided it was worth the thirty minutes Old Bob had promised she'd save.

She fiddled with the radio but couldn't find any music she liked, so she shut it off and turned onto the trail, clicking her high beams on once she got going. The last thing she needed was to hit a deer out in the middle of nowhere.

After about ten minutes she noticed a second moon rising from behind the trees.

*What the...?*

She checked her rearview mirror to make sure no one was behind her, then stopped the car and got out. Hadn't Old Bob's "visitors" reported seeing two moons? Shelly smiled and shook her head. She was letting his story get to her. It had to be some sort of atmospheric illusion, the moon's reflection bouncing off the clouds somehow, right? Taking a deep breath, she stood for a minute longer, scanning the valley below. *A valley?* This was farm country; it was flatland for at least a hundred miles in every direction from town. She didn't remember seeing anything like this on the map. And hadn't Old Bob said this road was flat the whole way?

Just what the hell was going on?

As she got back into the car, the radio turned itself on, and the sudden burst of static made her jump. When she reached to turn down the volume, the static stopped, and she heard her own voice coming from the radio, telling her not to take the shortcut.

*"Please, stay off the Eris Ridge Trail!"*

She snapped the radio off. "That's it, I'm getting the fuck out of here!" she said, her voice too loud in the suddenly claustrophobic car interior. She checked her rearview mirror again to see if it was okay to turn around, when she saw the first creature. Shaped like a person but bent low to the ground, hands in the dirt, pale skin glowing under the moonlight. She couldn't see any eyes, only a mouth with far too many teeth. *Sharp* teeth. As she watched, two, three, then four more of the creatures emerged from the darkness, skittering toward her car. The way they moved reminded her of a pack of wolves stalking their prey.

"Fuck this!" She threw the car into drive and tore off down the trail, leaving a cloud of gravel dust in her wake. Overhead, one of the moons winked and smiled. Its laughter echoed across the valley...

# CHAPTER TWO

"Koko, I don't think we're in Colorado anymore."

Erik didn't know how long they'd crawled through the darkness in the tunnels beneath the hotel. Or how far they'd traveled. He only cared about one thing: that he'd been reunited with the best friend he'd tearfully said goodbye to three months earlier. He'd held his eighteen-year-old dog Koko in the vet's office as the life had left her tired old body, cradling his sweet girl as she became a bag of bones.

An encounter with an ancient being at a writers' retreat in the Stanley Hotel had led to their reunion. Their reunion had led to their journey into the darkness beneath the hotel. And their long passage through the darkness had led them to this beach, here on an unknown sea. An impossible sea, considering they'd started their journey in the mountain town of Estes Park, Colorado.

But right now, none of that mattered. Because right now, he and Koko were back together.

Erik did have one regret, however: losing his phone.

When the battery had died as he'd crawled through the tunnel, he'd stuck it in his pocket, but it must have fallen out. Not that GPS would do him any good now, as he doubted any satellites were circling overhead. But the flashlight app sure would have been helpful, along with the camera to document their trip. Providing he ever found a place to charge it, of course.

He stopped walking and looked up to the night sky again. An alien sky, filled with millions of twinkling lights, in colors both familiar and indescribable. Worst of all were the black stars, darker than the night itself, tiny pinpricks in the firmament that allowed no light through, and which actually seemed to gobble up the surrounding glow, like visible black holes. Was he the first person to walk beneath these strange constellations? The thought was awe-inspiring and terrifying all at once.

He threw a stick down the beach for Koko as they resumed their walk. She had a spring in her step, as if she were three or four again, not the eighteen years she'd been when he'd said goodbye to her. With each throw, he expected her to slow down, but if anything, she was getting quicker, more energetic, as though she'd awoken from a long sleep. Which, when he thought about it, was pretty accurate. The being he'd met at the Stanley, who Erik thought of as the Canine Reaper, had shown him how Koko had refused to cross over that day in the vet's office, which didn't surprise Erik in the least. While Border Collies were known for their stubbornness, Koko had always taken it to a whole new level. Telling Death to pound sand was *so* Koko.

They stopped to watch an enormous creature break the surface a hundred yards out from shore. Koko barked but didn't leave Erik's side. Jesus, good thing he hadn't thrown the stick into the water. Although it did make him wonder —if she'd already beaten death once, could she beat it again? He hoped he'd never have to find out.

# CHAPTER THREE

Craig sat on the roadside, frozen, as Vaughn drove away. Had he really heard his own voice on the radio, warning him to not trust that son of a bitch? Overhead, the stars darkled, an endless sea of sinister jewels. He might have sat there forever, mesmerized, had the ground not started to shake.

He twisted around and saw an impossibly large shape towering in the distance. As he watched, its silhouette blocked out first one moon, then the other.

*A second moon? What the actual fuck?*

He remembered what Vaughn had said before stranding him out here, somewhere in the space between Nebraska and Colorado. *"Once, something so huge walked across the highway ahead of me, all I could see were its legs. The rest of it disappeared into the clouds. Ground shook like an earthquake every time it took a step."*

Craig couldn't gauge how far away Vaughn's beast was, but that giant mofo was getting closer.

He'd spotted a sign for the Eris Ridge Trail when Vaughn had coasted onto the berm. It was a rutted dirt path that angled off forty-five degrees from the highway. Without a second thought, he jumped to his feet and ran, rock shards peppering his legs like buckshot as he went, the creature in pursuit. It was slow, but with a stride so massive, Craig knew it would catch him, eventually. He needed to find a place to hide.

Forty yards down the trail, the air grew thicker, more humid, condensing and threatening to hold him in place. His ears popped as he pushed ahead, and suddenly he was through. The sky flashed white, and everything changed: a blinding sun, high overhead, scrub brush dotting the landscape on both sides of the trail. He spun and looked back. The creature was gone but the ground was still shaking, so he ran deeper into the ever-shifting scenery... palm trees now, salty air... onward down a cobblestone street, past a row of empty houses... Craig stole a glance over his shoulder in time to see a house disappear beneath a hoof the size of a U-Haul truck.

The beast was back.

The sky darkened and storm clouds raced over a green cheese moon as he ran past a sign welcoming him to Walpurgis County. Another bolt of lightning revealed a bridge spanning a churning black river. Pale white crabs larger than Golden Retrievers scrabbled over each other below, searching for a way up the riverbank.

The road became gravel, then dirt, and led into a forest; the branches formed a canopy overhead. Calves burning, Craig sprinted into the leafy tunnel. The path emerged from the forest onto a six-lane highway, a massive traffic jam of abandoned vehicles with names he'd never heard of, like a Takuro Spirit. A small town's skyline shimmered in the distance. A road sign read "Circadia 19 miles." He picked his way through the gridlock, climbing over cars when there was little space to navigate between them.

The smell of ozone preceded another bolt of lightning, and the freeway was a dirt road, thick rows of corn on each side. The farther he ran, the closer the corn grew to the road, until the road itself was just another row. A turn to the left, through the cornrows, and he emerged onto a rocky ridgeline. To his right, prairie grass; to his left, a hundred feet below, an obsidian beach, green seafoam leaving cryptic patterns in the sand with each wave. Far offshore, a leviathan breached the surface and started making its way toward the land.

He headed into the grasslands. Smoke on the horizon. No, not smoke. A sheet of rain. Black rain. Lightning arced from cloud to cloud, illuminating hundreds of shadowy figures skittering toward him. He turned back toward the ridge, only now the sea was gone, replaced by rolling foothills that led to snow-covered peaks.

Into the foothills he ran, racing through an empty village, passing dry stone walls and cottages with thatched roofs. The path widened into broken concrete, yellow grass growing between the cracks... A half mile on either side of the road, rust-covered robots ten stories tall towered over the cornfields. Skeletons hung from their upraised metal arms, slowly swaying in the breeze. The *screech* of rusted metal-on-metal made his hair stand on end.

He ran. Faster, this time.

# CHAPTER FOUR

"Don't you ever get tired of eating these?" Wayne asked Sammie when she dropped another of the six-legged rodents at his feet. It was the third such creature she'd caught that afternoon, and he knew by the way her tail thumped against the log he was sitting on that she'd be happy to catch as many as he could cook.

The rodents, which he'd dubbed squixels, were a big part of the reason he and Sammie weren't enjoying steak and beer with their neighbor, Chuck. If she hadn't found that first skeleton near the Delain Gulch trailhead back in the Arapaho National Forest, he'd never have found the overturned sign for the Eris Ridge Trail. And if he hadn't found that sign, they never would've ended up here, lost in the place he'd come to think of as the "Far Beyond," as in *far beyond* normal.

He had no idea how long they'd been lost in the wilderness. Time operated differently here than it did in the real world. Back before his phone had died, he'd somehow still occasionally been able to talk with his friend Chuck in Idaho Springs. He'd learned that what felt like an hour here was days back there. What felt like days here were months back home. It scared him to think about how much time he'd have lost if he ever did make it back. Maybe they'd finally have those flying cars he'd been promised as a kid.

Things had been pretty disorienting when they'd first come through the portal. When he wasn't looking, his surroundings would change, from a mountain ridge to an ocean beach, in the blink of an eye. They'd walked through deserted frontier towns, passed under iron giants with bodies hanging from their arms, picked their way through traffic jams of abandoned cars, hiked alongside an over-grown monorail track, and spent several nights in the various Koko gas stations that dotted the landscape. He'd traveled most of America when he was younger, but he'd never come across a station with a black Border Collie for a mascot before.

The changes had slowed once his cell phone finally died. He figured there was a connection, that the anomalies had something to do with electronic interference. This world—or worlds, depending on how you wanted to look at it—was unstable. Electricity exacerbated that instability. Sure, there were still times when he'd turn around to see the landscape had changed, but those were the exception now, no longer the rule.

The one constant, though, was the utter lack of people. As far as he could tell, he was the only living person on the Eris Ridge Trail. *Signs* of civilization were everywhere. Once, they'd come across the remains of an enormous statue, like something from a medieval fantasy novel. It had human legs, but only four toes on each sandaled foot.

And of course, there were the skeletons hanging from those metal monstrosities.

Truth be told, he didn't mind it. Much. Sure, he missed

Chuck, but for the last three years, since a drunk driver had killed his wife, Lori, he hadn't had much use for the company of his fellow man. As long as he could spend time with Sammie, he was happy.

And Sammie, well, she loved it here. Back home, she'd been showing her age, and her arthritis had been getting worse, a common health issue in Australian Shepherds. Some days it was all she could do to jump in and out of his Jeep. But out here on the Eris Ridge Trail, it was as if her clock had been turned back a dozen years. Her coat was shinier, she had a new spring in her step, and her eyes hinted at an intelligence far beyond that of a normal dog. Yeah, Sammie had adapted to life on the trail just fine. Would she revert to her older self if they somehow made it back? He wasn't sure if he was willing to take that chance.

Wayne pulled his knife from his backpack and started skinning the squixels Sammie had caught. Once he'd field-dressed them, he put the meat on sticks and stuck them over the fire he'd built when Sammie had been out hunting. They were scary looking things—six legs, two extra rows of jagged teeth—but they tasted like chicken. What he wouldn't give for some salt and pepper. Maybe some crushed red pepper flakes. And a beer.

He sighed. *A beer would really hit the spot right now.* At least he had clean water. He made sure to collect some whenever it rained, and topped off his canteen from the lakes and streams they passed. He always boiled it, just in case. After taking a long swig, he poured some into Sammie's silicone bowl, which she immediately emptied.

"That's enough for now, girl," he said, scratching her behind the ear. "Why don't you take it easy for a bit while I cook dinner? You've earned your rest today."

Sammie lay down next to his feet. She let out a long,

contented sigh, and within a few minutes she was snoring away.

Wayne turned the skewers, then leaned back on his log. They'd been on a stable section of the trail for a couple of weeks now, working their way toward a mountain range that didn't seem to be getting any closer. Whether this was because the mountains were huge or the landscape was stretching as they went, he didn't know. Not that it mattered. It was a goal, and goals were good to have.

The wind picked up a bit, blowing sparks from the fire. He moved the skewers up so the meat wouldn't burn, then studied the sky. Far away, toward his left, the clouds had turned the color of an angry bruise. As he watched, they grew darker still, and a bolt of lightning arced across the sky. He figured they probably had an hour, maybe two, before the storm reached them.

He nudged Sammie with his foot. "Wake up, buddy. We need to eat and then find some shelter. Looks like a storm's coming."

# CHAPTER FIVE

After walking through the night and what felt like the better part of a day, the cliffs along the beach had flattened enough that Erik was confident he and Koko could make their way up from the shore.

He had spent the last couple of miles looking for a safe place to climb when he came across a trail sign for the Eris Ridge Trail. A narrow path wound its way through the trees.

"Maybe we're not the only ones here after all, Koko," he said. "Let's go see what kind of trouble we can get into."

Koko tore along the path, leaving a cloud of grit and pine needles in her wake. It reminded Erik of the time he and Koko had gone camping in Rocky Mountain National Park a few years before the writer's retreat. A park ranger at the visitors' center had told him about a trail across the road from the Stanley, which was just a few miles outside of the park. He'd also told Erik to go left at the fork to avoid the Eris Ridge Trail. Running across a sign for the very same trail here, that couldn't be a coincidence, could it?

"Slow down, girl!" he yelled. The climb wasn't quite as easy for Erik. There were no steps, only tree roots and rocks. He was sweating through his shirt when he rounded a bend and saw Koko sitting at the top of the trail, waiting for him to catch up, her tongue out in a happy grin. "Almost there, buddy."

She barked, as if to say, *Hurry up! You need to see what's up here!*

Erik's jaw dropped when he finally reached the top. He stepped out of the forest and onto a two-lane asphalt road.

*What the hell?*

It felt exactly like that day they'd exited the trail across from the Stanley years ago, except there was no hotel here. No mountains, either. Just dusty plains as far as the eye could see.

He looked back to see if they'd missed a directional sign, but the trail was gone. So was the forest, for that matter.

"Maybe I bumped my head down in the tunnel a little harder than I thought," he said. Puzzled, Koko tilted her head and gave Erik a *What the fuck, dude?* expression.

He shrugged. "Your guess is as good as mine."

He looked right, then left. The sun was a little lower in the sky toward his right, which, back home, at least, would indicate west.

"We might get a little more daylight if we go in that direction, Koko. What do you think?" Koko barked and trotted off down the road. "Okay, west it is."

*The dog in black fled across the desert, and the wordslinger followed.* Erik laughed at his own joke.

They might have been walking through a desert, but with the temperature, it felt more like the mountains. If anything, it was a bit chillier here than Estes Park. He was glad he'd worn a hoodie on the ghost tour he'd taken that last night in the hotel. It would have been nice if he'd thrown on a pair of jeans instead of cargo shorts, but at least he had on his good hiking boots. He only wished he'd stuck a few protein bars and his water bottle into one of his empty pockets.

There was no vegetation, save for a few tumbleweeds being blown around by a stale breeze. Just miles and miles of dust and sand. It wasn't long before grit coated Erik's mouth and nostrils, which only made him thirstier. When they stopped for a quick break, he patted Koko, and a cloud of dust puffed up from her coat. Her tongue was hanging far out of her mouth now, and this time it wasn't from excitement. They needed to find water, and soon. He knew they were up against the Rule of Threes for survival: you could go three minutes without air, three days without water, and three weeks without food. In extreme conditions, the rule expanded to include three hours without shelter. They'd been lucky so far, weather-wise, but he wanted to find something sooner rather than later, since he didn't know what the night would bring.

Finally, after what seemed like several more hours—*why hasn't the sun moved?*—a smudge appeared on the far horizon. A small hill, the tip of a distant mountain range, or maybe, with any luck, a town.

Erik picked up the pace. "Come on, Koko, let's get a move on." Twenty minutes later, he realized it wasn't a town, but a lone gas station. Its sign had fallen over in the parking lot, fortunately missing the two pumps.

He breathed a sigh of relief. He didn't want to get his hopes up about food or water, but at least they'd have shelter for the night.

Koko ran ahead, excited about the chance to explore something new. She was waiting by the front door when Erik finally caught up with her, where a hanging sign read, "Welcome to Koko's Convenience Store #42." Above the words was a large photograph of a black dog with a red collar.

It wasn't just any black dog with a red collar, though. It was Koko. *His* Koko.

Her picture was also above the gas pumps, on the sign that had fallen over, and in the store windows, too.

It seemed impossible. No, it *was* impossible, but it was also real. This gas station, and, according to the door sign, at least 41 others just like it, had his dog as a mascot. He felt a little like Charlton Heston at the end of *Planet of the Apes.* "Well, at least they didn't blow it all up," he said with a nervous laugh.

He reached for the door handle, not sure what to expect. Based on the fallen sign, broken canopy lights, and sickly yellow weeds growing from cracks in the concrete, the station had clearly been abandoned for some time now. Years, maybe, from the looks of it. To his surprise, the door was unlocked.

Inside, it looked like your typical American convenience store, except for the photos of Koko everywhere. There she was, sucking on the straw of an oversized fountain drink. There she was, above the drinks cooler, wearing a sweater. There she was, eating a loaded hot dog at the snack bar.

Most of the shelves were empty. They did find a few bags of jerky, which he hoped were still edible. A box of shriveled and definitely inedible Twinkies disproved the urban legend. No power meant the soda fountains wouldn't work. The ice machines were dry, the water long evaporated. The coolers were all empty, too. Next to the register was a small display of disposable lighters. Erik grabbed the last two and put them in one of his pockets. *I might find something in the back I can burn.*

The interior of the store had grown noticeably dimmer while they searched, so Erik stepped outside to see if the sun was finally setting. He held the door open for Koko, who padded out and lay down on the concrete. Amazingly, the sun still hadn't moved, but a line of dark clouds was building on the horizon. The wind picked up, and the sand stung Erik's face.

Twin bolts of lightning arced from cloud to cloud; the flash blinded him for a second. When he could see again, the desert was gone, and stubby pines dotted the land around the station. Erik sniffed the air. Under the ozone from the lightning was a familiar scent. It reminded him of a camping trip he and Koko had taken several years earlier in the mountains of New Mexico. It took him a few seconds to recognize it. "That's piñon, girl. Now we've got something to burn. Let's go get some wood before the storm gets here. We can try to sort out what just happened later."

Across the road, they reached the first piñon tree, which had dropped several needles and a few smaller twigs that would make good kindling. He arranged them in a small pile. "Remember that one," he said. "We'll pick up the kindling on our way back."

Koko nodded and peed on the bush.

They walked another ten yards to the next piñon tree. It had died, and several larger branches had fallen off. He snapped four more from the trunk and took those back to the kindling pile. It was enough for tonight, but he wanted to gather more wood before it got wet from the storm. Or disappeared again. They set off for the next bush.

After what felt like about thirty minutes, he had enough wood to keep a fire going for three, maybe four nights if he kept the flame small, though he still hadn't decided where to build the fire. *Indoors might not be a good idea, but it's better than having an open flame near the gas pumps.* He hadn't noticed many rocks when he was gathering wood, but he hoped he could find enough behind the building to build a small fire ring. He took Koko with him to go look.

As he turned the back corner, he caught a glimpse of something scurrying away from the store's rear door. It was fast, but Koko was faster. She caught it in her jaws and snapped its neck with three quick shakes of her head.

She pranced back over to Erik, clearly proud of her kill, and dropped it at his feet. It looked like a squirrel, but it had six legs. And way too many teeth for its mouth. There wasn't a ton of meat on it, but at least they'd have something to eat tonight.

Leaning against the back wall were several old steel wheels. *Yes!* He pumped his fist in celebration. He could build a fire pit with one of those. Now all they needed was water.

The back door was locked, so he started rolling the wheel toward the front of the building. They turned the corner and *clang!* the wheel hit something metal sticking out of the ground. Erik stepped around the overturned wheel and saw what he'd run into—a hand pump for a well.

"Someone is definitely looking out for us, Koko." He grabbed the handle with one hand and pushed. It didn't move. He wrapped both hands around it and pushed harder. Still nothing. He continued to push down as hard as he could, stopping only to wipe the sweat from his hands. Thirty seconds went by. A minute. Then two. He was about to give up when he felt the handle budge. He readjusted his grip, the excitement giving him a renewed burst of energy. The handle moved an inch. Then two. Finally, it broke free. He pumped it a few times and waited.

No water.

He continued pumping, faster and faster until sweat soaked through his shirt. Up, down. Up, down. Up, down, until water gurgled deep down in the pipe. He kept pumping. The gurgle turned into a burble, and suddenly water was gushing onto the cement.

He cupped his hands beneath the flow, catching a small amount. It smelled stale, but not moldy or dirty. Just to be safe, he wanted to find something to boil it in.

Koko had no such qualms, though, and lapped from the growing puddle. "Koko, no! Stop!" He tried to shove her away with his foot. She didn't move, and she didn't stop until the water from the pump had slowed to a trickle.

Not for the first time, Erik wondered if dogs could catch the same parasites from bad water that humans could. He'd seen Koko drink from some pretty questionable sources over the years—mud puddles, algae-coated bird baths, a creek that smelled like an animal had died in it farther upstream—and she'd never gotten sick. Still, he wasn't going to take any chances. He wouldn't run the pump again until he had a container he could boil the water in.

The wind had picked up and was blowing the smell of the coming rain down the road. For now, he wanted to get something to catch the rainwater in, maybe an old mop bucket or the grease traps from the hot dog rollers, at the very least. They wouldn't hold much, but beggars can't be choosers.

He continued to roll the wheel around the building and let it rest by the pile of wood and kindling.

"Let's get all this stuff inside, Koko, then get ourselves situated. Looks like we'll be calling this place home for tonight at least."

Thunder clapped, as if to reiterate his point.

Once inside, Erik locked the front door.

"Just in case," he said. "Just in case."

# CHAPTER SIX

The road that led Craig past the iron giants changed from rows of corn to the foothills of distant snow-covered peaks to a grassy meadow before the landscape stabilized, although he ran for another mile before he noticed. He slowed his pace from a run to a trot then stumbled and collapsed onto the fragrant, velvety grass.

His legs burned, his sides ached, and his breath came in ragged, hitching gasps. Eventually, he pulled himself into a seated position. The land behind him was clear. Free of the beast, at least. Storm clouds in the distance billowed up like smoke on the horizon. That, he could deal with. But had he finally escaped the beast that had been chasing him since Vaughn had stranded him... where, exactly? And *why*, for that matter?

Wherever this was, it wasn't his world. That alien sky had been proof enough. But where had the Eris Ridge Trail taken him after that? He couldn't have been hallucinating, could he? All the different places had bled into one another, as if realities were overlapping, like the thin spots in the spaces between that Vaughn had told him about. Or like one of the science fiction stories he spent so much time reading. Too much time, according to his ex-girlfriend. That was just one of the reasons she'd dumped him, which is how he'd ended up in a car with Vaughn in the first place. He shook his head, then slapped himself, once, twice, three times, each slap harder than the last, until he calmed down. He couldn't afford to lose his shit out here. Not if he was going to find a way back home.

First things first, though, he needed to find shelter.

Out of habit, he pulled his phone from his pocket and turned it on. He doubted the GPS could tell him where he was, but it was worth a shot.

To his surprise, the GPS locked in on his position. But the places displayed on the screen didn't match his surroundings. The map showed he was right up the road from a town called Clifton Heights. Should be within eyeshot, as a matter of fact. But as he watched the screen, Clifton Heights disappeared, only to be replaced by West Newton. He held the phone above his head and turned in a circle, trying to get the GPS to lock in on north. When he finished turning, he wasn't surprised to see the landscape behind him had changed again. The mountains were closer, and a lake shimmered in the distance. He stared at his GPS; now the nearest place was Estes Park. Wait, that was in Colorado! He walked toward the lake and the scenery changed again. The forest was now a vast plain of brown dirt and scrub brush. The GPS said he was headed toward Christmasland, which made him chuckle, despite his predicament. *Christmasland, in this desert?*

The arrow for north moved again. He held the phone up and turned to his left in a slow circle. As he did, the desert gave way to a snow-covered field. Light flurries stuck to his hair. He wasn't dressed for winter, so he was glad when the scenery shifted again. Now the GPS said he was close to a place called Circadia. He remembered seeing a sign for that when he'd been running from the beast. He took a step in that direction and found himself standing on an old two-lane road bisecting a barren plain. Broken wind turbines dotted the landscape, towering high above the dirt below. Blades had fallen off several of them, and it was obvious they hadn't been maintained for a long, long time.

One of the still-attached blades shifted, letting out a loud *screech*, just as Craig felt the ground beneath him tremble. Pebbles bounced up and down around his feet as the road shook again. Harder this time.

The beast lumbered toward him in the distance. *How is that possible?* As he watched, the monster stepped between a pair of turbines. Its spiky tail swung low and collapsed one tower in a cloud of ancient dust that billowed across the plain. With its next step, the creature crushed another blade in its path. Pieces of shrapnel flew through the air.

Craig shoved his phone in his pocket and took off running. The landscape changed. Now he was on a blacktop road heading directly into the storm.

Heavy sheets of rain pounded the pavement as the wind threatened to blow him off his feet. There was nowhere to hide from the storm or the beast, so he kept running. Maybe he could lose it like he'd done before.

The sky lit up with the biggest display of lightning he'd ever seen, and an immediate crack of thunder made him cover his ears. He couldn't hear himself scream.

The ground had stopped shaking, though. *Maybe that big fucker cut itself on one of those blades and is bleeding out somewhere back there!* The grin felt manic on his face.

This time when the landscape changed, Craig was shocked to hear a dog bark. It was running down the road straight toward him. Fast. Far behind it was a man trying to catch up. Craig didn't know what to do. What if the dog were feral? What if the man was working with Vaughn? He hesitated, but the shaking ground made his decision easy. Even if the man was aligned with Vaughn, he'd have a better shot at dealing with him than with the monster behind him.

He ran toward the dog. Behind him, the beast's wail echoed across the landscape, like the trumpets of Jericho.

# CHAPTER SEVEN

After a hurried meal, Wayne cleaned up their campsite and called Sammie to his side. "You ready to go, girl? We need to find a place to hunker down."

The storm clouds had continued to gather as they'd eaten, the sky darkening until it felt like early dusk.

It was going to be a rough one. Already, thunder was echoing off the hillsides. He just hoped it wouldn't bring a scene-quake, or, if it did, they'd at least be able to ride it out without incident. The landscape had stopped changing so frequently once his phone had died, but he knew massive amounts of electricity could also trigger the effects.

They hiked another couple of miles without finding shelter. Wayne was almost resigned to getting caught in the storm when he finally spotted a hole between a pair of boulders about twenty feet up the hill from the path they were on.

"Let's go check it out, Sammie, I think that may have to do." The dog ran up to the opening, then stopped and sniffed at the air coming out of the hole. She turned to

Wayne and barked, then disappeared into the cave. "Good enough for me," Wayne said, and followed her up the hill.

The cave's interior was dark but dry. Standing in the mouth of the cave looking out, Wayne could see the last few miles they'd hiked. A bolt of lightning struck a tree near where they'd just been, and as Wayne retreated further into the cave, Sammie leaned hard into his leg, shaking. "That was a little too close for comfort," he said. "Let's hang back here for a while."

Lightning flashed again, illuminating the inside of their shelter. When his eyes cleared, they were still inside the cave, but the forest was gone. Now they were looking down over two lonely lanes of crumbled blacktop.

The smell of the coming rain hitting the asphalt reminded Wayne of the time he and Lori and Sammie had been caught in a summer storm on their way back from the Dillon Reservoir near Silverthorne. They'd almost made it back to the campground when the rain had started, and were soaked by the time they finally reached their site. The couple had stripped off their wet clothing and huddled together in one sleeping bag, while Sammie snored in the corner. Wayne must have fallen asleep afterward because the next thing he'd known, the sun was out, and the tent was empty. He'd got up and stuck his head out the front flap. Lori was making a fire, and Sammie was lazily following the path of a butterfly—

Another flash shook him from his memories. Their cave had disappeared, along with the road. Now they found themselves in an endless prairie, making him the tallest thing for miles.

"Oh shit, Sammie, down!" They both flattened them-selves against the dirt, which was rapidly becoming a sea of mud under the torrential downpour. They were lower than the prairie grass now, but not by much. He hoped the next flash would transport them somewhere with a shelter.

He scooted on his belly up to where his head was even with Sammie's. "Okay, buddy, when the landscape changes again, we need to move. It's too dangerous to stay put any longer." He didn't know if it was a trick of the light, but he swore Sammie nodded in agreement. "You really do understand what I'm saying sometimes, don't you?" Sammie smiled. A flash of lightning reflected in her eye.

Now they were in a forest. The road was about ten yards away. Wayne was up and running deeper into the woods when he realized Sammie wasn't with him. She was standing where they'd appeared, her head cocked at an angle. He'd learned to rely on her canine senses, so he hurried back to her side.

"What is it, girl? You hear something? Smell something?" The only thing Wayne could hear was the storm, and the only things he smelled were the rain and the ozone. Sammie took a few steps toward the road, then stopped and tilted her head again, twitching her ears as she tried to home in on whatever she was hearing. Wayne followed her to the roadside. He heard something over the rain, too. The sound of a man screaming.

Sheet lightning illuminated the landscape. When Wayne's vision cleared, Sammie was running down the road toward a man who was stumbling in their direction.

The ground beneath Wayne shook, and the silhouette of a mountain towered in the distance behind the man.

*No, it can't be a mountain,* he thought, because it was moving.

# CHAPTER EIGHT

Later that night, Erik was sitting in the store, leaning against an end cap display he'd moved to give him a better view of the gas pumps and the parking lot. He'd found a plastic bucket in the back to catch the rainwater, and a smaller metal one that was perfect for boiling water.

He'd opened a small window high on the back-room wall to let out the smoke from the fire pit he'd made. Using a Leatherman multi-tool he'd found in a desk, he'd skinned the creature Koko had caught. She'd been drooling while it cooked. So had he.

Now, with a little food and water in their bellies, the effects of their reunion and the subsequent long walk were catching up to them. Koko had already curled up on a blanket he'd found in a closet. He could hear her snoring over the storm.

Lightning arced across the sky in colors he couldn't describe. Thunder shook the building hard enough he worried the glass might shatter. He shielded his eyes from a flash so bright it appeared to be daylight outside. Wait, it *was* daylight outside. And the landscape was all desert. It changed three more times as he watched over the next hour, from desert to lakefront to an empty medieval village, and back to piñon scrub. It was nighttime again. The only things that didn't change were the road, the station, and the storm, which was finally letting up enough that he felt safe opening the door a bit. He propped it open with a rock to let in some fresh air.

Koko lifted her head, sniffed, then went back to sleep.

Erik also drifted off, but woke with a jolt to the sound of the back doorknob jiggling.

Someone was trying to get in.

Erik ran to the back of the store. He flicked one of the lighters on.

"Hello? Is someone there?"

The door rattled harder.

Erik reached to unlock it, but Koko's growl stopped him. Her hackles were up, and she was baring her teeth.

Erik pulled his hand back. "Hello?" he asked again.

Still no answer.

*BANG!*

Something smacked the door hard enough to dent the metal. Erik and Koko both jumped. A shape passed by the upper window. Whatever was out there, it was tall. That window was at least eight feet off the floor. It was heavy, too. The walls shook as the shape lumbered around the side of the building toward the front, where one of the racks fell over with a loud crash.

*Shit! The door's propped open!*

Erik ran to the front of the store; Koko on his heels, barking the whole time. He kicked the rock out, pulled the door shut, and twisted the lock into place. They ducked back into the darkness. Erik pulled Koko tight against him, wrapping one hand around her muzzle.

"Quiet," he whispered, although there was no way whoever—or whatever—was outside hadn't heard her. Erik wondered if the smell from their meal had attracted it.

The footsteps rounded the corner of the building and then... they stopped.

They sat in the darkness and waited, but whatever had been out there was gone.

The rain had slowed to a light drizzle. The thunder and lightning were letting up, too.

Erik thought he heard a dog bark in the distance. Koko's ears perked up, and she tilted her head. If she'd heard it, that meant he wasn't imagining it. With her tail up, Koko pranced back and forth in front of the door as the barking grew louder, eager to see who was coming.

Erik pressed his face against the glass, his eyes darting about. He was contemplating going outside when a bolt of lightning hit the ground across from the station. He jumped back from the door and shook the spots from his eyes. Two men and a dog stumbled into the parking lot, looking over their shoulders. They ran for the front door.

Koko was going crazy now, with her front paws against the glass.

The younger of the two men pulled on the locked door. "Let us in, please! Hurry, before it finds us again!"

The older man put his hand on the dog's head. It was a black dog, about sixty pounds, taller and thicker than Koko, with one brown eye and one very, very blue eye. As it paced along the front window, Koko did the same from the other side. Slowly, they began to wag their tails. First in small circles, then bigger and bigger.

Koko jumped and hit Erik with her front paws. She barked, then gestured toward the dog with her nose. Just in case he wasn't getting the hint, she grabbed his hand in her teeth and pulled him to the door.

"What are you waiting for, man? Open the damn door!" The younger man was growing more agitated. The older man remained calm.

"How do I know we can trust you?" Erik asked through the glass.

"You don't," the older man replied. "But our dogs seem to trust each other, and that has to count for something, right?"

Koko hit Erik again, then jumped up and bit at the door handle. The only thing that kept her from opening it herself was the absence of opposable thumbs.

"Okay, Koko, don't make me regret this." Erik unlocked the door and let them in.

Koko and the new dog side-eyed each other for a moment, then the bigger dog sniffed Koko's butt. She stiffened, and then it was her turn. When she'd given the new dog a good sniff, both wagged their tails and started playing, until they padded off and lay down together in the corner near the front window.

"Sammie's not usually so quick to make friends," the older man said. "At least she wasn't, back where we're from. Course, yours is the first dog we've seen since getting lost here, so maybe she's different now. Sure acts different. Seems younger. Smarter, too."

"I know what you mean," Erik said. "Koko's been really different since... since I got her back. She went away for a while, but now she's better than ever." He grinned when Koko lifted her head at the mention of her name.

The older man stuck out his hand. "I'm Wayne," he said, "and that's Sammie."

Erik shook his hand. "Nice to meet you. I'm Erik and this is Koko."

Wayne took a closer look at Koko, then did a double-take. "What the hell?" He pointed to one of the many pictures of her on the walls. "Is this the same Koko?"

"I don't know how it could be. I adopted Koko when she was eight weeks old, and she was never part of any advertising campaign." He pointed to the picture on the front door. "But I can't deny that's her in the photos. I don't get it."

They turned to the younger man who'd come in with Wayne and Sammie. He glared at Erik, then Wayne, as if he couldn't decide whether to trust them. Finally, he shrugged and said, "Craig." He didn't offer to shake hands.

"We just met a little while ago," Wayne explained. "Sammie and I were trying to survive a scene-quake when—"

Erik held his hand up. "I'm sorry, a scene *what*?"

"Scene-quake. That's what I call it when the landscape changes so fast. It can go days or even a couple weeks without changing too much, but when it happens a bunch in a short time, I call it a scene-quake."

"Scene-quake." Erik tried the phrase out. "That's a pretty good name for it. We experienced a few of those when we got here. And a lot more tonight."

"They happened a lot more when we first got here, too," said Wayne. "But they calmed down once my phone died. I think the act of crossing over triggers them. Electronics, too. And lightning. Must be something to do with electricity."

"I think it's that monster," Craig said.

"What monster?" asked Erik.

"Huge fucking thing. Spiked tail, probably twenty,

twenty-five stories tall. Glowing orange eyes, with thick, wriggling appendages like stubby little tentacles." He shook his head. "It hurts my brain to think about it. Thing's been chasing me for who knows how long. Every time I thought I'd gotten away, it somehow caught up to me." He looked at Wayne. "Yeah, I know I had a phone with me, but I wasn't using it for anything. Well, except the last time, right before you found me. I'd been trying to use the GPS when it came back. So maybe you're on to something. Maybe not."

"What about you, Erik?" Wayne asked. "Did you notice your phone causing anything to happen when you used it?"

Erik grinned sheepishly. "Believe it or not, I don't have one. I mean, I did, but I lost it back in the tunnels beneath the hotel after the battery died."

"So how did you get here?"

"It's complicated, but long story short, Koko and I crawled here through a tunnel that started under the Stanley Hotel in Estes Park. I don't know how long we were in there, but eventually we ended up on the shores of a giant lake or maybe even an ocean. And I don't have to tell you there aren't any oceans in Colorado."

"Interesting. Sammie and I crossed over on a new trail we'd found in the Arapaho National Forest near Idaho Springs," Wayne said. "We'd been hiking and came across a sign for the Eris Ridge Trail." Erik and Craig perked up at the mention of the trail, but neither of them said anything. "Wait, you've heard of it?" Wayne asked. Both men nodded. "Okay, we'll come back to that in a second. Anyway, I'd been hiking that part of the forest for years, and I know there's no such thing as the Eris Ridge Trail. I would've seen it, either in person or on a map. But that sign was old, like it had been there for years."

"So you just started walking on it?" asked Erik.

"Well, yeah. How could we *not* check it out? Right, Sammie?"

Sammie woofed and wagged her tail.

"We've been lost here ever since. I call it the Far Beyond."

"How long ago was that?" Erik asked.

"I honestly have no idea. Here, it's probably been seven, maybe eight months, but back there? It could be years. Time moves differently on this side than it does back home. You'll see."

"How do you know time is different here?" Craig asked.

"Back when Sammie and I first got lost, I could still make the occasional call back home. Don't ask me how that worked. But whenever I talked to my friend, Chuck, I thought minutes or maybe an hour had passed. But he told me hours or days had gone by in Idaho Springs. Didn't believe him at first, until he texted me a picture of the local paper so I could see the date. That was the first time I thought we might be in serious trouble. The next time I talked to him, which was also the last, more than six months had passed over there." He shrugged his shoulders. "It gets even crazier, though."

"What do you mean?" Erik asked.

"Sometimes a day on this side feels like it lasts three days. And sometimes it doesn't even seem to last three hours. Nights are the same way. If there's a pattern to it, I haven't figured it out yet." Wayne hooked his thumbs through his belt loops. "So how long have you and Koko been here?"

"That's a good question. It was night when we came out of the tunnel, but the sun came up not long after. We walked along the beach for quite a while before we found a sign for the Eris Ridge Trail, which wound through a forest and led up to a road. It was daytime when we finally exited the woods. And then we hiked for what seemed like days until we found this place, even though the sun barely moved in the sky. You'd think part of one night and most of a day, that'd be what, fourteen, maybe sixteen hours?" He rubbed his chin. "But I can tell by my stubble it's been a lot longer than that. What about you, Craig?"

Craig pushed himself off the counter he'd been leaning against. "No idea. I've been on the run ever since that bastard Vaughn dropped me off somewhere in the space between Nebraska and Colorado." He narrowed his eyes. "That name mean anything to either of you? He picked me up in Omaha on some ride-share app that just showed up on my phone. Had some crazy story about the veil between worlds thinning out in the empty spaces between towns on the map. At first I thought he was pulling my leg, but the more he talked, the more I believed he believed it. Finally, he stopped the car in the middle of nowhere. I heard my own voice on the radio, telling myself not to go with him, so I jumped out. I looked back at Vaughn as he drove off and I swear his eyes were orange. Had to be a trick of the light, though, right?"

"You didn't notice that when he picked you up?" Wayne asked.

"He was wearing sunglasses, okay? I even made a joke about him being a Corey Hart fan, but he had no idea who I was talking about. That should've been my first clue some-thing was wrong with the guy." Craig snorted in disgust. "Anyway, he drove off and left me there on the side of the road in the middle of the night. The constellations were all... wrong. I didn't recognize any stars, and some of them actually seemed to be darker than the sky itself."

"That sounds like the sky near the water where Koko and I were."

"Then you know how much it fucks with your head. I'd probably still be sitting there staring at it if the ground hadn't started to shake. I turned around and saw this enormous creature in the distance, tall enough to block out the moon. Both of them." He snorted at Wayne and Erik's raised eyebrows. "I ain't ashamed to admit it. I panicked and got the fuck out of there. That trail you two mentioned, the Eris Ridge Trail?" Wayne nodded. "There was a sign for it right where Vaughn dropped me off. I ran down it trying to get away." He stopped for a moment. "And that's when things really went to shit."

"I forgot to tell you there was also an Eris Ridge Trail across the road from the Stanley," Erik said. "A few years back, on a camping trip in Rocky Mountain National Park, a ranger told me to stay off it, to take the other fork instead. We never got on it, but I wonder now if the tunnel we crawled through intersected it at some point?"

"Okay, that's interesting," Wayne said. "So, that's at least one thing we all have in common."

"Yeah, real interesting," Craig snapped. "How do I know you two aren't making all this up?" He paced as he spoke. "How do I know you're not working with Vaughn? Huh?"

"I can't speak for Erik, but if I were working for or with this Vaughn fellow, why would we have saved you? We didn't have to do that. We could've just let that thing catch you."

"Why did it disappear, then, right after I ran into you, huh? You're telling me that was just some sort of coincidence?"

"It disappeared because I turned your phone off. And the storm let up. I told you, those things are related."

Craig stopped in front of the empty drink coolers. He opened the door and slammed it shut, then stomped over to where Wayne was standing. He leaned in toward him. "Yeah, and I told you, that creature started chasing me before there was any storm!" Wayne stood his ground until Craig broke eye contact.

Sammie and Koko both lifted their heads. Their tails had stopped wagging.

"Hey, let's all just take a deep breath and calm down, okay?" Erik stepped between the two men. "None of us really understand what's going on here, and this isn't helping. We need to trust each other if we're going to find our way home."

"What makes you so sure that's even possible?" Craig asked.

"I don't know if it is. But based on everything that's happened over the past few days, and the way I got Koko back at the hotel, I'd like to believe anything is possible."

"That's the third time you've said you got Koko back," Wayne said. "What do you mean? Did she run away?"

"You won't believe it."

"Try me."

"Because Koko died three months ago. That's why I think anything's possible."

"What kind of happy horseshit are you trying to pull?" demanded Craig. He threw his head back and let out an exaggerated sigh. "Morons! I've got morons on my team."

Koko moved to Erik's side. She stared at Craig, unblinking.

"Yeah, come on, Erik," said Wayne. "How did Koko die three months ago? She's clearly alive now."

"Just hear me out, okay?" Erik took a moment to collect his thoughts. "My job had transferred me from Colorado to

Texas. Koko and I both hated it there. She was getting really old, and the Texas heat wasn't doing her any favors. On top of that, she had what the vet called 'Doggie Alzheimer's.' She'd started experiencing night terrors and lost control of her bowels. It was no way for her to live, and I couldn't stand to see her suffer like that. It was time to say good-bye." He reached down and scratched Koko's head. "I was with her when she took her last breath."

"The next few months were hell for me. I went to the Stanley for a writers' retreat, a chance to reset my life."

"What do you write?" Wayne asked. "My wife and I used to read to each other before bed."

"Horror stories."

"Gee, I wonder what your next book will be about?" Craig stomped to the front of the store and stared out the window.

Erik paused. "Anyway, I kept dreaming about Koko the whole time I was there. I mean, really vivid dreams. One night, I dreamed I heard her in the hallway outside my room. I tried to follow her down to the lobby, but I tripped on the stairs and twisted my ankle something awful. I finally found her in the bar, where I met... the Canine Reaper." He rolled his eyes in embarrassment. "Yeah, I know what it sounds like. But he showed me what he saw that day. He was in the room with us to help her cross over. And he said she'd refused to go, that she had unfinished business.

"The next morning, I thought it had all been a dream, of course. Except that my ankle was black and blue."

"You had to have been sleepwalking, right?" Wayne asked.

"I don't know." He rubbed the back of his neck as he spoke. "I'd tripped down the stairs *in my dream*, but my ankle was actually swollen in real life. How does that happen?"

"Because you were sleepwalking, duh." Craig smirked.

"Maybe? But that night, during a ghost-hunting tour, Koko was waiting in the tunnels beneath the Stanley. The ghost hunter warned me against following her, but I had to. She was, I mean she *is*, my best friend. So, I crawled into the tunnel after her. No idea how long we were in there, although it was long enough for my phone battery to die. Eventually, we ended up on that beach I told you about. An impossible beach in Colorado, I might add."

Wayne rubbed his temples while Craig stared at the floor.

"Look, I know it sounds crazy, all right?" Erik continued. "But is it any crazier than what we've gone through to get here?" He looked at Craig. "A stranger with glowing orange eyes drops you off in the 'space between worlds,'"— he made air quotes as he talked—"and then you get chased by some Lovecraftian nightmare?" He turned to Wayne. "And you found a trail you *knew* didn't exist? And now Sammie's getting younger and smarter? And don't get me started on these 'scene-quakes'! How is any of that less crazy than the Canine Grim Reaper giving me and Koko a second chance?"

"Well, when you put it that way..." Wayne chuckled.

Erik wasn't finished. "So I guess you'll just have to forgive me if I come off as a bit too Pollyanna about our present situation," he said. "But taking all things into consideration, yeah I do think we might find our way out of here. And I think Koko is the key. She must have come back for some reason, right? Why can't that reason be that she had to rescue you two? She's already rescued me."

# CHAPTER NINE

Wayne had enough jerky in his pack for everyone to have a piece, including the dogs. "That's all I have," he said, handing Sammie the last piece. "You're gonna have to catch some more squixels tomorrow, okay?"

Sammie nodded as she chewed.

"See," said Wayne, "that's what I'm talking about. I swear she understands what I'm saying to her now."

"Of course she understands," Craig said. "Dogs understand 'sit' and 'stay,' don't they?"

"Tricks are learned behaviors," Wayne said. "This is different."

Erik bent down and rubbed Sammie's head. "I get it," he said. "Koko was always a smart dog, up until those last few months. But now she's *really* smart, like a-dog-in-a-Dean-Koontz-novel smart."

"Great. Maybe we should put them in charge," Craig said, shaking his head. "Can't do any worse than listening to you two."

Wayne stiffened. He hoped he wasn't going to regret bringing Craig along. "You got a problem, Craig, just say it."

Craig rolled his eyes, then walked behind the counter and started tapping the glass. "Fine. My problem is, we're stuck in a gas station in the middle of nowhere, I mean *literally* nowhere, with pictures of this guy's formerly dead dog plastered all over the place. Can either of you explain that?" He jabbed his finger at the two men.

Wayne looked over at Erik, who shrugged.

"See? And I bet neither of you can explain what's happening to the landscape, either. Those... what did you call them?"

"Scene-quakes," Wayne said.

"Yeah, those scene-quakes." Craig waved his hand dismissively.

"I think—"

"I know what you think," Craig interrupted. "It's our phones. Or the lightning."

"Or maybe it's the creature, like *you* said," offered Erik, trying to keep the peace.

"Yeah, or maybe it's the creature. Maybe it's all three. Maybe it's none of them. My point is you don't know. When you get right down to it, you don't really know much of anything. Especially considering how long you've supposedly been here." He glared at Wayne, who rubbed his jaw.

"I know this much," Wayne said. "You'd be dead if Sammie and I hadn't saved your ass."

Craig opened his mouth, but Wayne cut him off before he could speak.

"And I know all three of us would probably be dead if Erik here hadn't taken a chance and let us in."

"Well, in all honesty, you can thank Koko for that," he said. "I was still on the fence."

"Then thanks, Koko. We owe you our lives." Wayne took a sip of water, willing himself to keep his cool. He hated confrontations, but Craig was really pushing his buttons. "And I know we're safe here tonight. The storm's moved on, the scene-quake's stopped, and the creature that was chasing you is gone." Wayne glared until Craig broke eye contact.

Erik cleared his throat. "And I know Koko and I are exhausted. I say we all just try to get some sleep for now. We can talk about our next steps in the morning." He turned to Wayne. "You think someone needs to keep watch?"

Wayne thought for a moment then shook his head. "I think we'll be okay here for the night. Everything has quieted down outside, and these Koko stations seem to be little safe houses. Sammie and I have spent more than a few nights in them with no problems." He stretched and cracked his back. "If it makes you feel any better, I'll probably be up for a little while anyway, so I can keep an eye on the door."

Erik nodded. "If you think we're safe, that's good enough for me. Koko and I are gonna lie down in the back and try to get a little sleep." Koko followed him through the *Employees Only* door.

"Are there any blankets or pillows?" Craig asked Wayne once they were gone.

"You think this is a slumber party?" Wayne laughed. "You wanna braid my hair?"

"I was just—"

"Relax, I'm just busting your balls." He slid his backpack across the floor to Craig's feet. "You can use that for a pillow if you want. I'll rest my head on Sammie."

Craig's eyes widened in surprise at Wayne's gesture. "Uhm, thanks. For everything." He fidgeted with his shirt-tail. "Look, I'm sorry about earlier, okay?"

Wayne decided to let it go. "Don't worry about it. It's been a rough night for all of us. Now try to get some sleep, okay?" He settled down next to Sammie. She was already snoring.

# CHAPTER TEN

I t'd been three days, more or less, since they'd left the Koko station. They hadn't known which way to go that first day, so they'd waited for the sun to rise and headed in the opposite direction. "Better to have it on our backs in the morning," Wayne said.

"But won't that mean it's in our faces in the afternoon?" Craig asked. He wondered if Wayne might be pulling his leg as payback for the way he'd acted the night before.

Wayne laughed. "Not necessarily. Remember how I told you time runs differently here? So does the sky. The sun doesn't always follow a straight line across it. And if you pay attention, you'll see that sometimes the clouds go in a line opposite the direction of the wind, almost like they have a mind of their own, or they're being pulled by something. Bottom line is, we can't assume the sun will set in the west like we're used to." He studied the clouds for a moment, shook his head, then spat on the ground. "I swear, sometimes it seems to set in the same place it rose from. Just wait, you'll see."

Fortunately, the sun had behaved itself so far,

traversing the sky in the same direction and giving them more daylight than night. At least that's how it seemed. It was hard to tell without a clock. Craig wanted to check his phone, but Wayne had taken it from him at the Koko station and wouldn't give it back. "Is it really that important to know what time it is?" he'd asked when Craig had balked at his refusal. "Important enough to take a chance on bringing that creature back?" Craig kicked a rock down the road and marched ahead. They hadn't known each other long, but he already resented the way Wayne treated him like a child sometimes.

Near the end of the third day, a bump appeared on the horizon. Within a few miles, they could tell it was a small frontier town, the kind you'd see in an old Western. Erik whistled the theme to *The Good, the Bad, and the Ugly* as they walked down the main street.

"Nice," Craig said. "I'm clearly the Good, and Wayne's the Bad—"

"Which makes me the Ugly?" Erik laughed.

"You said it." Craig cleared his throat and switched to a passable Clint Eastwood imitation. "You see, in this world, there's two kinds of people, my friend. Those with loaded guns and those who dig. You dig."

Erik laughed. "That's pretty good." He stopped and looked around. "Hey, do you think this place looks like the town from *High Plains Drifter*?"

"Maybe a little," said Wayne.

"Well, except for one major difference." Craig chuckled. "Nobody's painted it red. Yet."

It might not have been an exact replica from a spaghetti western, but it was still a stereotypical ghost town. They'd counted a restaurant, a saloon, a general store, a post office, a two-cell jail, and a blacksmith's as they'd made their way down the main strip, along with a handful of private residences. They didn't bother checking out the other streets.

They stopped in front of the town's only hotel.

"Unless we want to keep exploring, I'd say this place looks as good as any," Wayne said. "What do you guys think?"

Craig studied the building from his position on the street. The sign above the front door simply read "Hotel." It was a small, two-story structure. Wood siding. Windows with the old wavy glass that made everything look a little distorted. Storm shutters the same color as the siding, which was the same color as the dirt that coated everything in town. He made his way around the back to have a look. When he returned, Wayne and Erik were already inside.

"Couldn't find anything with indoor plumbing, huh?" Craig asked as he walked through the front door. "At least there's a shitter out back."

"Sorry."

"Ah, well, it's better than sleeping on the ground again," Craig said. "I call dibs on the bed if there's only one."

That turned out not to be a problem. The hotel had four bedrooms. Three upstairs, and one at the back of the first floor, which they decided was where the owner of the hotel would have slept. The lower level also had a small lounge with a couch and two chairs, and a dining table with four wooden chairs. There was no kitchen.

Craig ran his finger through the dust on the table. "Looks like someone forgot to call housekeeping," he said.

"I saw a pump when we first got into town." Wayne

picked up an old wooden bucket sitting by the front door. He held it above his head, then inspected the sides. "Doesn't look like there's any holes in it, so I guess I'll go see if that pump works while you two get settled in. Who knows, we could end up staying here for a bit." He snapped his fingers. "Come on, Sammie. Maybe you can catch us some dinner while we're at it." She stretched and followed him out.

Craig watched them through the window. Once they were out of earshot, he turned to Erik. "I don't know about you, but there's something I don't trust about him."

Erik closed his eyes and sighed. "What are you talking about now?"

"I can't put my finger on it. Maybe because he always has an answer for everything?"

"No, he doesn't. He has an educated guess for everything, because he's been here the longest."

"Fine. But if he's been here for so long, then why *doesn't* he have answers instead of guesses, huh?"

Erik shook his head. "What is wrong with you?"

"What's wrong with me? Are you serious? Doesn't it seem odd to you that he's so at ease with all this? It doesn't bother him that we're lost out here in... what did he call it, the 'Far Beyond'?" Now it was Craig's turn to make air quotes.

"Maybe he's more accepting of it because he's had time to adjust," Erik said. "You ever think of that?"

"Not really, but I have thought about how quickly you take his side on everything."

"Oh my god, you need to relax, okay? Why don't you go upstairs and lay down for a while? I think it'd be good for *all* of us."

Craig took a deep breath, filled his cheeks with air, then

blew it out. "Yeah, you're probably right," he said. "I'm sorry if I sound paranoid. I'm just all by myself out here."

"What are we, chopped liver?"

"No, I mean, you have Koko, and Wayne has Sammie. I don't have anyone. Even back home I was alone. My girlfriend dumped me, which, looking back, was no big surprise. That's why I took a ride with Vaughn. Just needed to get out of Dodge for a while. And look where that got me." Craig's guts twisted when he remembered how Vaughn hadn't understood what "get out of Dodge" meant. Or how he'd never heard the song "Sunglasses at Night" by Corey Hart. Or any of the other half dozen red flags he'd ignored. How could he have been so trusting?

"I'm sorry to hear that, and sorry you feel that way," Erik said. "I was alone a few months too, after Koko died."

"She really died, huh?"

"Yeah, she really died."

"Fucking crazy, man."

"Yeah, fucking crazy."

Craig bent down and held his hand out to her. She gave it a perfunctory sniff, followed by a quick lick. Craig laughed. He'd always been more of a cat person, but he liked Koko's spunk.

"That's better than a lot of people get," Erik said. "She can be a little standoffish when you first meet her."

Koko bowed her head and let Craig scratch her behind the ears. The tip of her tail thumped the floor.

"My ex-girlfriend's cat was the same way." Craig stood up and cracked his back. "I don't wanna push my luck with Koko too much, so on that note, I think I will go lie down for a bit. You'll come get me when Wayne gets back, right? You won't leave me here? Promise?"

"Promise," Erik said. Koko nodded in agreement.

Craig walked up the stairs to the second floor, then stopped. "Hey, Erik?"

"Yeah?"

"I think you need to come up here a second."

"Everything okay?"

"Just come up here, please?" He paused. "And bring Koko."

# CHAPTER ELEVEN

E rik patted his leg, a gesture for Koko to follow him. *There's always something with this guy,* he thought as he headed up the stairs. Craig was standing at the top of the landing, not moving.

"Okay, what's so important that we needed to come up—"

Erik stopped mid-sentence. When they'd explored the hotel earlier, the stairs had ended at a small landing with doors to the three bedrooms. Now, however, the landing branched off into two long hallways that stretched and curved out of sight, with closed doors on alternating sides of the corridor. The top third of the walls were covered in yellow pine paneling that had been popular in the 1960s. The bottom two-thirds were decorated with light blue tiles from the same era. The floor was a checkerboard of black and white linoleum squares. Muzak played from large speakers in the walls, the kind you'd see in a high school classroom. Buzzing fluorescent lights hung from the ceiling.

Erik looked left, then right, then left again. He opened his mouth and then shut it.

"I know, right?" Craig said.

Koko made a small whine in the back of her throat.

"Those are fluorescent lights," Erik said. "And that's Muzak we're hearing. In an abandoned ghost town."

"Yeah."

"That means there's power coming from somewhere. But there haven't been any scene-quakes..." He scanned the walls for a switch. He didn't see one. Didn't see any outlets, either. "What should we do?" he asked.

Craig didn't say anything.

They stood there for a few moments. Finally, Craig started walking down the corridor to the left. Erik followed him while Koko stayed on the landing.

Craig stopped at the fourth door and put his hand on the wood. "It's warm," he said, and reached for the handle.

Erik grabbed his arm and pulled it back. "Don't," he said. "We should wait for Wayne."

Craig shook off Erik's hand and opened the door.

Erik shaded his eyes from the blinding sunshine. Desert sand spilled into the hallway, the heat forcing them to take a step back. In the distance, a ridge formed in the sand. It turned in their direction. Something was tunneling underneath the surface and racing toward the door. When the mound was about twenty yards away, segmented insect legs the width of tree trunks burst from the ground—

Craig slammed the door.

He tried the next one.

It opened into another hallway almost identical to the one they were standing in, with the same 1960s decor and alternating doors. But instead of curving, it stretched straight ahead for about twenty feet. Erik blinked, and the hallway was fifty feet long. He blinked again and couldn't see the end of the hallway. It struck him that if he stepped through the doorway, he'd wander that hall forever. He reached past Craig and pulled the door shut.

By now, curiosity was getting the better of him, so Erik picked the next door. It opened into pitch blackness. The lights above them flickered and buzzed, as if the darkness were feeding off them. Koko immediately started to bark. A leathery, rustling noise whispered from somewhere deep in the void, the sound of something slowly unfolding. They covered their ears against a growing, high-pitched screech.

Erik grabbed the handle and threw the door shut, but not before two bats the size of racoons flew into the hallway. They circled his and Craig's heads, grabbing at their hair, then zipped toward Koko and the staircase.

Erik yelled at her to watch out, but she stood her ground. While the first bat was too high for her to reach, her eyes locked onto the second, which flew lower and slower. When it got closer, she jumped and caught it between her teeth. The bat's screech as Koko shredded its body sounded almost human. It took Erik and Craig only a few seconds to reach her, which was more time than she needed to kill it. She dropped the mangled creature at Erik's feet, then looked up at him, smiling.

"Jesus, what if it had rabies?" Craig asked.

Erik grabbed Koko's face and checked for bites or scratches. She was clean.

"It didn't bite her, so she should be okay," he said. "I don't think you can get it from biting something that has rabies. It's transmitted through their saliva. Besides, she's up to date on her shots." He paused. "Well, she was, before..."

"Shit, she came back from the dead, man. She's probably immune to *everything* at this point."

Craig bent down for a closer look at the bat. "Hey, aren't bats supposed to be pretty much blind?"

"Yeah."

"Then how do you explain that?"

Icy fingers crept between Erik's ribs, squeezing his heart. "What the actual fuck?" The bat's eyes were human, and the same shade of blue as Sammie's. Its mouth had so many teeth they were bursting through its lips and cheeks.

"Jesus, look at its hands!" Craig turned and retched.

The bat's hands were human, too, small like a child's, with long, sharp talons instead of fingernails.

Erik lifted his foot and stomped on its head. One of its eyes popped out, but the optic nerve kept it from rolling away. Blood and brain matter splattered the wall. Koko sniffed at the eyeball, but stopped when Erik told her *no*.

"I'm going to take this outside and get rid of it." Erik picked up the broken body and carried it down the stairs, holding it at arm's length.

"I'll be down in a second," Craig hollered after him.

Erik had just come back inside when Koko started barking. He heard Craig scream once, followed by a slamming door. Koko's barking grew more frantic.

"Shit!" He ran up the stairs, taking them two at a time. Koko was jumping up and down, pawing at one of the doors.

Craig was gone.

Erik grabbed the handle, but hesitated. He knew he should go through and try to help Craig, but he let go of it and stepped back against the far wall, shaking.

He was still standing there a few minutes later when Wayne and Sammie ran up the stairs.

"We heard Koko barking," Wayne panted. "We got here

as fast as we could." He looked around at the hallways. "What the hell? This wasn't like this before..."

Erik shook his head.

"Where's Craig?"

"He's in there." Erik pointed at the door across the hall.

"What's in there?"

Erik wouldn't meet Wayne's gaze. "I don't know. I was downstairs, getting rid of something Koko had killed. It looked like a giant bat, but it had human eyes and hands. Another one escaped before she could catch it."

Wayne waved him off. "But what about Craig?"

"I heard him scream, then a door slammed. I got up here and Koko was pawing at the handle, trying to open it."

Wayne stared down at him. "So, you just stood there? Why didn't you try to help him?"

"I thought it'd be better to wait for you and Sammie. If I went through there, you'd never know where we were."

"Koko could've told us," Wayne said.

"Yeah, I guess." Erik lowered his voice. "Look, I was afraid, okay?" God, he hated feeling like this. "I'm not brave like you."

Wayne took a deep breath. "It's all right. We're here now. Let's go." He went back downstairs and grabbed all their gear. He put his pack on, then handed the rest of their meager belongings to Erik before he opened the door and stepped through, Sammie and Koko close on his heels.

Erik hesitated for a moment, then followed them inside.

# CHAPTER TWELVE

Craig waited until he'd heard Erik leave, then went back down the hallway. One of these doors had to lead back home.

He opened four in quick succession. The first led to an ice cave. Snow-capped peaks were visible through the cave opening. There were no mountains in Nebraska, so that was a no.

The second opened into the hull of a great wooden ship. Watching the walls sway up and down triggered his seasickness. Nebraska was landlocked, which ruled that one out.

The third led to the burnt-out ruins of a drive-in theater, blackened cars scattered across the lot. Someone had erected three crucifixes near the concession stand. Sun-bleached skeletons hung from them. Even if that was Nebraska, it wasn't *his* Nebraska.

The fourth opened into a serene, dark forest. He took a moment and listened to the peaceful sounds of the night: crickets, peepers, the hoots of an owl. There weren't a lot of forests in Nebraska, but there were plenty in Colorado.

Maybe this would lead back to where Wayne or Erik had come from. He inhaled, savoring the damp, earthy smell of decaying leaves. Wherever this was, it was autumn.

*"Craig,"* a voice whispered in the darkness.

He cocked his head. Had someone just said his name? He listened again.

*"Craig."* The voice sounded fainter this time, as if it were moving away.

He stepped through the door and listened.

*"Craig."*

Behind him, Koko growled.

He shushed her and took another few steps into the woods. "Hello?"

*"Craig."*

It was closer now. Koko barked.

"Quiet, Koko!" He turned to see the door swinging shut. He'd gone too far into the woods. "Shit, shit, shit, no!" he yelled, knowing he wouldn't reach it in time.

He screamed for help as the door closed, then disappeared.

He was alone in the forest.

*"Craig."*

No, he wasn't. The voice was much closer now. Too close. It circled through the trees. First to his left, then behind him, and in front. Always whispering. How could it move that fast?

*What if there's more than one of them?*

He tried to put some bass in his voice. "Who are you? How do you know my name?" The night swallowed his words.

*"Craig."*

Something crawled out from behind a large pine tree.

*Shit.*

It was one of the creatures he'd seen when he was running from the beast. Man-shaped, low to the ground, pale white skin. No eyes. And far, *far* too many teeth.

*"Craig,"* it whispered, running its tongue over its teeth. Blood dribbled down its chin, a splash of scarlet against its alabaster skin. It smiled as it licked the blood from itself, then tilted its head and whispered his name again.

Craig ran.

*"Craig!"* the creature screamed and gave chase.

Moonlight illuminated the forest, which was the only reason he didn't run headfirst into a tree. The light also eliminated any chance of hiding, though, while the blanket of dead leaves crunching under his feet killed any opportunity for stealth.

If he wanted to live, he'd have to outrun it.

He stole a glance over his shoulder. He'd had a thirty-yard head-start on the creature. It was down to twenty now.

*"Craig!"*

He feinted left, then zigged right.

The creature matched his moves.

Fifteen yards away now.

*I don't want to die, not here, not like this!*

He turned back to the left and ran into a small clearing. There, on the far side, were several large rocks surrounding a crooked tree. Craig ran as fast as he could, legs pumping, the creature now so close he swore he could feel its breath on his neck. Straight up the rocks he ran, planting his foot on the tree trunk and jumping into the air. He twisted and stretched, and his hands latched onto one of the tree's lower branches. He pulled himself up and scrambled higher into the tree.

Below him, the creature howled in frustration. It skittered across the rocks and put its front hands on the trunk, but it didn't follow him.

*It can't climb!*

"Yippie-ki-yay, motherfucker!" Craig laughed. He slipped and almost fell out of the tree. The creature jumped, but he pulled his foot up in time.

They faced each other.

The creature couldn't reach him. But he couldn't get out of the tree. *Stalemate.* How were the others going to find him?

*What makes you think they'll come looking for you?* whispered a small voice in his head.

"Shut up!" he said. He wanted to slap himself, but was afraid to let go of the trunk.

*They're not coming. You were a jerk and they're going to leave you here to die.*

"That's not true!" he whispered through gritted teeth. "Erik promised he wouldn't leave me."

*"He was ly—"*

"Craig!"

A familiar voice yanked Craig out of his head. That had sounded like Wayne. But how could he be sure it wasn't another creature?

"Craig! Where are you?" Was that Erik? They *had* come looking for him!

The creature's head snapped around in the direction of their voices. At the sound of Koko and Sammie barking, it hissed, then skittered off into the woods.

# CHAPTER THIRTEEN

L eaves crunched underfoot as Wayne led Erik,
Sammie, and Koko into the woods.

Wayne looked back at the doorway they'd just come
through, which was set into the base of the largest tree he'd
ever seen. Fluorescent light spilled into the forest. The
impossibility of it all made his head hurt.

He pulled an orange ribbon from his pack, tied it around
a sapling about twenty yards from the door to mark their
way back, and yelled for Craig.

When there was no answer, Erik shouted, too. Sammie
and Koko took turns barking.

Still nothing. They kept walking.

Sammie stopped and sniffed the air, then Koko joined
her. They both turned left and picked up their pace. Wayne
stopped and tied another orange ribbon around a low
branch of one of the smallest trees. He closed his pack and
trotted after the others.

They took turns yelling as they went. Wayne tied more
orange ribbons to mark their way. Finally, Craig answered.
"Over here!"

"We're coming!" Wayne shouted. "Keep talking so we can follow the sound of your voice!"

"Wayne, Erik, listen to me!" Craig shouted back. "I'm in a tree at the edge of a clearing. There are creatures in the woods that can imitate a human voice. Don't listen to them. Only listen to me!"

"How do we know it's really you, then?" Erik yelled.

"If I was one of them, would I have told you that?"

Erik raised his eyebrows. "That's a good point."

"Ask me something only I'd know!" Craig's voice was louder now. They were getting closer.

"How did you end up here?" Erik yelled.

"Some asshole named Vaughn abandoned me on the side of the road!"

"How did we first meet?"

"Some asshole named Wayne rescued my dumb ass and then Koko made you let us into the gas station!"

They followed Craig's voice for a few more minutes. By the time they reached the clearing, he was telling them about the disgusting bat Koko had killed.

When they were halfway to the tree, Craig climbed down and ran over to them. He gave Erik a huge hug. "Man, am I glad to see you guys! I wasn't sure if you'd come looking for me or not."

"I told you we wouldn't leave you, didn't I?" Erik smiled and gave Craig a playful shove.

Wayne put his hands up. "So I'm an asshole, huh?"

Craig lowered his gaze. "Yeah, but you're our asshole."

"I can live with that." He pulled Craig in for a big bear hug.

When Wayne finally let him go, Craig bent down and gave the dogs a hug. He stood up and stared into the woods. "How did you know which door to go through?"

"Koko told us," Wayne said.

"And we all came through as soon as we could, right Wayne?" Erik added. Wayne hesitated, then nodded in agreement. No sense in telling Craig that Erik had frozen.

"I don't know how to thank you." Craig wiped his eyes. *Is he actually crying?* Wayne wondered. "I was starting to think I was on my own again."

"You can start by telling us about this thing that chased you," Wayne said. He needed to know what they were up against.

"Right." Craig touched a finger to his chin before speaking. "For starters, it's not the first one I've seen. I skirted a field full of them when I was running from the beast, before you found me. They're shaped like people, but they run on all fours. The way they move, it's like a bear, but also like an insect." He bent down and imitated their movements as best he could. "Their skin is bone-white and glows in the moonlight. No eyes. And way too many teeth. Like that bat Koko killed." Koko wagged her tail. "It ran off when it heard the barking."

"That's good," Wayne said. He made a mental note to slip Sammie and Koko some extra treats when they got back to the hotel. "Hopefully that thing will leave us alone on the way back."

Everyone was on high alert as they crossed the clearing and entered the woods. The moonlight made it easy to trace their way back. The dogs didn't seem to sense anything out of the ordinary, so Wayne felt good about their chances.

He untied the ribbons as they went, until there were only two left. "Okay, we turn here," he said. "We should see another in about twenty yards, and then the door will be another twenty yards or so from there. It opened out of the biggest tree I've ever seen. It's impossible to miss."

They reached the last ribbon and turned toward the tree.

The doorway was gone.

# CHAPTER FOURTEEN

Craig sprinted up to the tree and ran his hands over the bark. "Well, that's just fucking great! Game over, man. Game over!"

Erik grinned. "*Aliens*?"

"You know it. Best movie ever." He turned to Wayne. "Very funny. Now where's the door? I want to get out of here."

"I'm not kidding around. It was right there." Wayne pointed to the base of the tree.

"Well, it's clearly not there now!" Craig started to pace. "What the fuck are we gonna do?"

Wayne held his ground. "Why are you asking me?"

"Oh, I don't know, maybe because you've been here the longest? Because you're supposed to have all the answers?" Craig rubbed his temples.

"I've been on the *other* side of that door the longest," Wayne said. His words were clipped, his voice low. Craig was worried he'd pushed him too hard this time. "But we're not on that side anymore, are we?" Wayne continued. "Now we're on *this* side of the door, thanks to you. And I don't have a fucking clue how things work over here!"

"Guys," Erik whispered.

"In fact, technically you've been in these woods longer than any of us." Wayne poked Craig in the chest. "So why don't you have any answers?"

*Yeah, definitely pushed him too hard*, Craig thought.

"Guys!" Erik whisper-shouted this time.

"What?" Craig and Wayne snapped in unison.

"We have company."

One of the creatures was crouching a short way down the trail, sniffing the ground. Koko and Sammie growled.

"Stay," Wayne and Erik said at the same time.

"If it could sneak up on us without the dogs noticing—" Erik started.

"—we could be in serious trouble," said Wayne.

"It's too late to worry about that." Craig pointed to the creature's left. Another one had crept out of the woods. As they watched, another emerged to its right. Then another. And another. Heads raised, all five sniffed in their direction.

"How can they see us without eyes?" Erik whispered.

Craig considered this for a moment. "Maybe they're like bats? I mean, like regular bats, not the ones here with human eyes."

Koko and Sammie's growls intensified, their hackles raised. Craig didn't think they'd hold their stay much longer.

Erik glanced over his shoulder. "I don't see any of them behind us."

"Yet," said Wayne. "We need to move before they have a chance to surround us."

Erik and Craig nodded.

"On the count of three." Wayne raised his hand.

"One."

The creatures began to spread out.

"Two."

They inched closer.

"Three!"

Craig took the lead, Wayne and Erik in the middle, Sammie and Koko bringing up the rear.

*"Craig!"*

*"Wayne!"*

*"Erik!"*

The creatures howled the men's names as they chased them.

"Keep going, don't look back!" Craig yelled. He didn't know if the others could hear him over the sound of their frantic retreat through the crackling underbrush and dead leaves. He glanced back for a split second and instantly wished he'd followed his own advice.

The pack had spread out and there were at least eight of them now. If even one of the creatures managed to get in front of them, they were finished. Koko and Sammie at least had a fighting chance, thanks to their teeth and nails, but the men had no weapons other than their hands and feet, and maybe a stick if they could grab one in time.

*"Craig!"*

Behind them, the creatures continued to gain ground.

*"Wayne!"*

They were used to hunting in these woods.

*"Erik!"*

They knew the terrain.

*"Sammie!"*

The men were running without direction, stumbling over tree roots, slapping at branches that snagged their hair and clothes.

*"Koko!"*

"There, up ahead, I think I see a way out," Erik yelled. The men surged forward with a renewed burst of energy.

Craig broke through the trees and stumbled onto an asphalt road, Erik on his heels. To their left, a half mile away, a car was bearing down on them, its headlights illuminating the road ahead.

Craig jumped to his feet and waved. "Holy shit, guys, there's a car coming!"

Wayne and Sammie staggered out of the woods.

Erik grabbed Wayne's shoulders. "Where's Koko?" he screamed.

"She's coming!" Wayne said, panting. "She was right behind us."

The car was a quarter mile away now. It wasn't slowing down.

Craig and Wayne stood in the middle of the road, waving their arms and jumping up and down. Erik stared into the woods, waiting for Koko. Craig was worried he might run back in.

The driver finally saw them and slammed on the brakes. The tires squealed as the Subaru slid forward across the blacktop, stopping just a few feet away. Wayne slammed his hands onto the hood. "Please, you have to help us!"

The driver hesitated for a second, then reached over and threw open the passenger door. "Hurry, get in!"

Wayne and Sammie jumped in. Wayne reached behind him and opened the back passenger door.

"Craig, Erik, come on!"

"Not without Koko!" Erik ran back and forth, waiting for her to come out of the forest.

Craig stood in the road, frozen, memories of Vaughn

flooding his mind. He couldn't bring himself to get in the stranger's car.

Wayne yelled at them again to get in.

*"I said, not without—"*

A terrible, sudden howl cut Erik off.

Craig knew it was Koko. He grabbed Erik and dragged him toward the car. "We have to go!"

Erik pulled free of his grip just as a round, black shape arced out of the trees. It smashed into his chest, knocking him back a step.

Koko's head tumbled to the ground, where it landed with a *squelch*.

Erik ran his hand through the blood on his chest. Craig saw his eyes widen as the realization sank in. Erik collapsed to his knees and fell forward. Craig managed to catch him just before his head hit the pavement next to Koko's. Wayne jumped out of the car and together they dragged Erik across the road and into the back seat. He didn't resist.

*"Koko!"* the creatures howled in unison.

"Drive, drive, drive!" Craig shouted as he pulled Erik's feet in.

The woman punched the gas, the sudden acceleration slamming the back door shut as they screamed off into the night.

# CHAPTER FIFTEEN

S helly floored the Subaru. It bogged down for a second and she was afraid she might have flooded the engine, but then it picked up and the car zoomed away from those —*things*. Whatever they were, they looked like the same creatures who'd trapped her on this road not long after she'd left Old Bob's a few hours ago.

She did a quick inventory of her new passengers. The older man in the passenger seat had knocked her notes and tape recorder onto the floorboard when he'd jumped in. He had a big black dog, an Australian Shepherd maybe, sitting in his lap. In the backseat were another two men. One, probably in his twenties, was staring out the rear window, watching those things play with whatever it was they'd thrown at the other man. *It couldn't have been a dog's head, could it?* The second man, who looked to be in his mid-thirties, was curled up and non-responsive. *Is that blood on his chest?*

"What the hell are those things?" she asked the man in the front seat.

He rubbed his temples, then tried to shift in his seat, a

difficult task with the dog in his lap. "Sammie, you need to get in the back, okay?"

Shelly swore the dog nodded before it hopped into the back seat. The younger man sitting behind Shelly scooted over to give Sammie enough room.

"I don't know what they are." The older man sighed and wiped sweat from his brow. "But if you hadn't stopped, they'd have killed all of us."

"Was that—" Shelly hesitated. "Was that a *dog's head* that hit him?" She nodded toward the second man in the back seat. He still hadn't moved.

"Yeah, that was Koko, his dog," the older man said, his voice low.

"Jesus." *What the hell had she gotten herself into?*

"I thought we were done for back there," he said. "So thank you. You saved our lives. My name's Wayne, by the way. The dog is Sammie. That's Craig and Erik in the back."

She caught Craig's eyes in the rearview and nodded. "I'm Shelly," she said. She looked toward Erik. "He okay?"

"I don't know. Those things just killed his best friend." Wayne's voice cracked. "I don't know what I'd do if it had been Sammie."

"I'm so sorry." She stole another glance in the rearview to make sure they weren't being followed. "What *are* they? I saw some earlier this evening, about three hours ago. They're the reason I'm still on this stupid trail."

Wayne's eyes widened. "Trail?" He snorted. "Let me guess, this is the Eris Ridge Trail?"

"Yeah, how'd you know? You guys from around here?"

Craig stuck his head between the front seats. "Lady, we have no idea where 'here' is."

"Well, here *was* near Wabash Plains, Indiana. Now, though?" She shrugged. "I haven't lived there long, but long enough to know the place shouldn't have things like that roaming the countryside." She leaned forward and pointed up through the windshield. "Doesn't have two moons, either."

"Two moons?" Craig laughed, then leaned back in his seat. "That might be the most normal thing I've seen in a while."

Shelly checked all the mirrors again. The creatures didn't seem to be following them.

Wayne stared out the rear window for a moment, then turned back to Shelly. "They're fast, but I doubt they can keep up with a car. We're probably safe for now."

"Probably?"

Wayne shrugged. "So how'd you end up on the trail?"

Shelly gave them an abbreviated version of her interview with Old Bob and how he'd told her the trail was a shortcut. "Something about it felt off," she said, "but it was late and the chance to cut thirty minutes off my drive home was too good to pass up. And look where that got me."

"I'm sorry to hear that, but we're certainly glad you did," Wayne said. "Still, I can't believe he'd tell someone to take this trail." He paused. "Unless maybe it's harmless in his world?"

*His world?* Shelly's reporter-brain put a pin in that statement. Something to follow up on later.

"Well, he did put in a disclaimer," she said. "He told me it should be safe because it was a full moon." She cocked her head forward. "Guess he wasn't counting on two of them."

"It sounds like we have a lot of catching up to do," Wayne said. "But if it's okay, I can't talk any more right now. I need to sit with this for a bit."

Shelly nodded. "I got half a tank of gas, so we're good for a while."

"Keep your eyes open, maybe we'll run into another Ko—" Craig stopped mid-sentence. Shelly tried to catch his eyes in the rearview, but he wouldn't meet her gaze. She put a pin in that, too.

"Why don't you two rest for a bit? You have a lot to process."

Wayne leaned his head against the passenger door window. "Yeah, we do. Thanks."

It wasn't long before Wayne and Craig were sleeping. She wasn't sure about Erik.

She replayed the events in her head. Someone—it turned out to be Craig—had stumbled onto the road. Erik, Wayne, and Sammie were right on his heels.

Erik had refused to get into the car, though, screaming for Koko, telling the others he wouldn't leave without her. But something had hit him in the chest. Something her mind *still* couldn't accept was a dog's head.

If she ever made it off this trail, this was gonna make one hell of a story. Definitely front-page material. Providing she could get her editor to believe it, of course.

# CHAPTER SIXTEEN

E rik was vaguely aware of the conversation going on around him. He'd been drifting in and out of consciousness since they'd thrown him in the backseat after Koko—

*Her head spiraled through the air, crimson drops spraying outward as it tumbled toward him...*

What was the point of being reunited with Koko only to have her ripped away from him again so quickly? He wished she'd never been brought back at all!

*The rotation of her head seemed to slow as it neared his chest. Her tongue lolled lifelessly from her slack jaws, her eyes glassy and dull...*

No, that wasn't true. Because the time they'd spent together these past few days made up for the time they'd lost before. She'd been her old self again, not the shell of herself she'd been when he'd said goodbye to her the first time.

At least he'd got to say goodbye the first time.

*The thud when her head hit his chest, obliterating his heart.*

*The heaviness of his arms when he tried to catch her head after it ricocheted off him...*

This time, the opportunity to say goodbye had been stolen from him by those things. They'd ripped her head off and thrown it at him. An act of cruelty he couldn't comprehend. He'd seen it coming toward him, but didn't believe his eyes. Even after it had hit him in the chest, he didn't believe it. *Couldn't* believe it. Not until it landed on the road and her blood sprayed over everything—

Oh god, he was covered in blood. Koko's blood. He needed to wash it off!

No, he didn't. He needed to sit here, perfectly still, and remember her. Honor her. She gave her life protecting them. Her pack. She'd sacrificed herself so they could live. She could have run ahead of everyone and got away. But she and Sammie had stayed together at the back, protecting the pack's rear flank, allowing him and Wayne and Craig to escape.

It was such a Koko thing to do.

He wished he'd been able to pick up her collar at least. To have something to remember her by. But Wayne and Craig had tossed him in the car so quickly.

They'd gotten away, but at what cost? His heart was still back there in the woods, with Koko's broken body.

And it always would be.

# CHAPTER SEVENTEEN

Wayne rubbed the sleep from his eyes. It was light out, which meant Shelly had probably let them sleep for a while. He wasn't upset, though, as he'd clearly needed the rest.

But now that he was awake, there was so much to do. They needed to check on Erik. They needed to talk about what had happened. Figure out their next steps. And how did Shelly fit into everything? He'd seen plenty of abandoned cars, but hers was the first one that actually worked.

*Wait.*

A working car meant electronics. Electronics meant—

"Pull over!" he shouted.

Shelly jumped and jerked the wheel. "What? Why?"

"I said pull over. It's not safe to be in a moving car!"

"Dude, relax, we're fine," Craig said. "We've been driving all night and nothing's happened."

Wayne spun around and glared at Craig. "How long have you been awake? Why did you let me sleep?"

"Because you needed it, man. We're almost out of gas anyway, so it's not gonna matter much longer. We saw a sign a few miles back for a..."—he paused—"...a K station, but we both know the tanks'll be empty. I think we should lay low there for a few days, give ourselves a chance to regroup. Give Erik some time to process things."

"How is he?" Wayne nodded down at Erik, who was still curled in the fetal position. It looked as if he hadn't moved all night.

"The same," Craig said. "He opens his eyes every now and then, but nobody's home."

"I can't imagine what he's going through." Wayne lowered his voice. "How it feels to have lost her again—like *that*—after just getting her back."

"What do you mean he got her back?" Shelly asked. "Was she lost?"

Wayne gave her a sad smile. "In a sense. It's a long story."

"I'm a reporter," Shelly said. "I love stories. And it looks like we're going to have plenty of time to share them."

Wayne turned and stared out the passenger window. Flat plains gave way to foothills, distant mountaintops dotted the horizon. They passed another sign for the Koko station. If it weren't for that bitter reminder they were still in the Far Beyond, this stretch of road could almost have passed for home.

The Subaru's engine sputtered and hitched.

"That's not good." Shelly sighed. "The gauge has been on E for a while now, but I didn't want to believe it. Normally, I'd just wait for someone to give me a lift to the nearest station or call AAA. But out here...?"

Wayne nearly jumped out of his seat. "Call AAA? Do you have a phone?" *Why didn't I think to ask earlier?*

"Do I have a phone?"

"Yeah, a cell phone. Do you have one?"

Shelly laughed. "Like a car phone? Of course not. Do you know how much reporters make? I'm lucky to have a quarter for the phone booth most days."

Before Wayne could ask her if they still had phone booths in Indiana, the engine died. They coasted for a few seconds and rolled to a stop about twenty yards short of the Koko station.

# CHAPTER EIGHTEEN

S helly followed Wayne and Craig to the front door. "What's if it locked?" she asked.

Wayne smiled and held it open for her. "They're never locked. There's never much in them, either, but they're safe."

"Safe from what?"

"Scene-quakes, for one."

"What's a scene-quake?"

"It's an easier thing to experience than explain," Wayne said. "Just wait."

"Is it okay to leave Erik out there?" Shelly nodded toward her car.

"He'll be okay," Craig said. "I rolled the windows down. Sammie's out there with him. I'll check on him in a bit."

"So what happened to him last night?" she asked. "Was that really a dog's head that hit him in the chest?"

Wayne nodded. "That was Koko," he said. "Like I said, it's a long story, and one I don't feel up to sharing right now."

"Okay."

Nobody talked for the next few minutes as they took stock of the station's interior. It reminded Shelly of the new convenience stations that were popping up around Indiana, only much nicer, with larger coolers, bigger display cases, and far more shelves. It had obviously been abandoned for a long, long time. She pointed to one of the many pictures of Koko, the store's mascot. "Cute," she said. "Isn't that the same name as Erik's dog?"

Craig nodded.

Wayne hadn't been lying about the store's inventory. The back room was empty, too. They returned to the front of the store. Wayne and Craig leaned against the counter. Shelly jumped up and sat on the spot where the condiments would've been.

After another few moments, she couldn't take the silence any longer. She could tell they didn't want to talk about Koko, so she pointed at Craig's earrings. "Not to change the subject, and I don't mean to be rude, but are you a queer?"

Craig's jaw dropped. "Wow! Apropos of nothing, but where did that come from?"

Shelly blushed. "It's just, well, I've never met one before. Not a lot of them in the middle of Indiana."

"Oh, you'd be surprised!" Craig laughed.

Shelly decided she liked the sound of his laugh.

"But no, I'm not. Why would you think that?"

"Because your ears are pierced."

Craig and Wayne both shared a laugh over that one.

Shelly felt her face flush again. "What's so funny?"

"I think I know what's going on here," Wayne said. "But I'm not sure you're going to like it. How old is your car?"

Shelly chewed her bottom lip. Was Wayne trying to trick her? "It's brand new. My dad bought it for me as a graduation gift. He was afraid of me driving all over the countryside by myself, especially in winter, so he got one with that new four-wheel drive. He's a bit overprotective. But what's that got to do with anything?"

"And you really don't know what a cell phone is?"

"No, I've heard of a car phone, but not a cell phone. Is that bad?"

Wayne smiled. "Shelly, what year do you think it is?"

"It's 1978. Like I said, I just graduated and landed my first job as a reporter for the *Wabash Plains Chronicle*. I know nobody's heard of it, but my working there is actually a pretty big deal." She sat up straight. "Not to brag, much, but I'm the first female reporter they have on staff. There have always been women who work there, sure, but all they do is answer the phones and other secretarial stuff. I'm the first one with a byline. *Story by Shelly Perkins*. That's me."

"Well, I hate to break it to you, Shelly Perkins from Wabash Plains, Indiana, but it's 2024," Craig said. "And you won't believe the things people get pierced now. Ears, noses, lips, tongues, nipples, even..." he pointed to his groin, then hers.

Shelly's eyes widened. She turned to Wayne. "He's putting me on, right?"

"No, he's not. People really do get their nipples and... other things... pierced."

"Duly noted. But I meant about what year it is."

"No, he's wrong on that one. It's actually 2020. At least it was when I crossed over."

Craig's eyes widened. "Well, this just got even more interesting."

"Yeah, I guess we never really talked about that, did we?" Wayne asked. "Don't know why I assumed we all came from the same time."

Shelly leaned forward. "Hold up. So all the weirdness from last night aside, you're also telling me we're from different years? Can I quote you on that?"

"If we ever get out of here, sure," Wayne said.

"Okay, Wayne, help me out on this," Craig said. "We came through a doorway back in our part of the Far Beyond, where we all thought it was 2020-*ish*, right?"

"Yeah."

"And now we're in a totally new place, where Shelly here thinks it's 1978."

"It *is* 1978."

"Fine, fine. That means if we make it home from *here*, it'll most likely be around 1978-ish. And that means we'll have jumped back in time over forty years."

Wayne opened his mouth, then shut it again.

The front door opened, and Erik walked in.

"Are you okay?" Wayne asked.

Shelly hugged him tight. "I'm so sorry about what happened last night."

"Yeah, man, if there's anything we can do, or if you need to talk..." Craig added.

Erik shook his head. "This might sound weird, but... Koko died last night, right? I didn't just dream that, did I?"

"I'm sorry, man, it wasn't a dream. Look at your shirt and your legs." They were covered in dried blood.

"Yeah, that's I thought," Erik said. He waved his thumb over his shoulder toward the front door. "It's just that..." he trailed off.

Shelly headed for the front door. In the side parking lot, Sammie was playing with a smaller black dog. "There's two dogs out there," she said. She stared at the new dog for a few seconds. "And one of them looks just like *that* one." She pointed to the picture of Koko on the front window.

Everyone ran outside. Koko and Sammie were chasing each other around the parking lot. Koko saw Erik, sprinted over, and jumped up into his arms. Her collar jingled when he caught her, and she covered his face in kisses.

"Koko came back to me!" Tears streamed down his face faster than she could lick them away. "Again."

# CHAPTER NINETEEN

Wayne hadn't believed Erik's story about Koko's first resurrection, although he'd wanted to. Erik seemed like a good guy. Sammie liked him, and he trusted his dog's judgment. He wasn't happy that Erik had frozen up when Craig disappeared, unable to do anything until Wayne and Sammie got there, although he couldn't hold that against him.

Erik had had no reason to lie about Koko dying, but come on... The Canine Grim Reaper gave your dog back to you? That was a bit much, even out here in the Far Beyond. And this had supposedly happened back in the real world, *before* they'd crossed over.

This morning had changed everything, though. Now he knew Erik was telling the truth. He'd seen it firsthand. He'd heard Koko's death howl. Seen her head hit Erik in the chest. And watched those things play with it in the road as they'd sped off. No, there was no denying it. Koko had died last night. This morning, she was alive.

Craig joined Wayne at the front of the station. "Can you believe that shit?"

"I can now."

"Yeah, I wasn't sure before either. I mean, I believed *Erik* believed it, but thought maybe he'd bumped his head too hard in the tunnels. But now...?"

Together, they watched Erik check Koko over for cuts and scrapes for at least the fifth time. He'd yet to find a single scratch. Whatever had brought her back had healed everything. Wayne wondered if she remembered what had happened to her.

"Shelly, you wouldn't happen to have any food in your car, would you?" he asked. "Maybe some bottled water?"

"Bottled water? Like Perrier?"

"Sure, that would work, if you have it."

Shelly snorted. "Again, do you know how much reporters make? I'm not buying a bottle of water when I can get it for free from a garden hose."

Craig laughed. "You see any garden hoses around here?"

"No, but come on, buying water by the bottle? What's next, you gonna tell me you have to pay for air to put in your tires?"

"Well, now that you mention it..."

Shelly playfully punched him in the arm.

Wayne was happy to see Craig and Shelly getting along so well. Craig had been overly suspicious of him and Erik, but he'd latched onto Shelly right away. It was good for him to form a bond with someone. Wayne had Sammie, and Erik, well, Erik was definitely bonded to Koko. It'd help Craig and Shelly a lot if they could lean on each other.

"It's okay," Wayne said. "Most of these Koko stations have a water pump out back. They really are a lifesaver."

"Anyone want to fill me in on how Erik's dead dog is their mascot?" Shelly asked.

"*Previously* dead dog," Craig corrected. "And your guess is as good as ours."

"Hmm."

Wayne knew she was filing that away for later. But right now, he needed everyone to focus on the present. "I was thinking we could empty out your windshield wiper container, clean it, and fill it with water," Wayne said. "There are plenty of streams and lakes where we can refill it, too, so we should be okay. I'd like to get going this afternoon, or tomorrow morning at the latest."

"I don't know, man," said Craig. "Maybe we should hang here for bit and chill. Some R&R might be just what the doctor ordered. Besides, it'll give us all a chance to get to know each other a little better."

Wayne thought about it for a moment. "That's actually a good idea. These last few days have been pretty much non-stop." He looked around. "All these trees, Sammie and Koko should be able to catch all the squixels we can eat."

"Squixels?" Shelly stuck out her tongue in mock disgust. "Do I even want to know?"

Craig laughed. "All you need to know is they taste like chicken."

"Chicken sounds divine right about now." Shelly licked her lips.

"Then it's settled." Wayne clapped his hands and patted Craig on the back. "We'll take the dogs hunting, load up on some protein, then figure out our next steps."

Craig pointed to Erik. "Should we ask him what he thinks?"

Wayne watched Erik rolling on the ground with Koko and Sammie. "I think he'll be fine with it."

Over the next few days, everyone grew closer. Shelly offered to clean the blood from Erik's clothes as best she could. She used a little peroxide from her first-aid kit and scrubbed them on a rock. Next, she tried flinging wet mud over the remaining blood spots, letting it dry before flaking it off to try to camouflage the stains. It only sort-of worked, but Erik told her he appreciated the effort.

They ate as many squixels as Sammie and Koko could catch, until everyone was too full to eat any more. Even the dogs must have reached their limit, because Wayne watched them ignore a few scampering across the edge of the parking lot.

It turned out Shelly wasn't kidding when she told them her dad was a bit overprotective; the back of her wagon was filled with stuff they could use. Besides the first-aid kit, there was also a 100-foot section of rope, a fold-up saw, a large Buck knife, a flannel blanket, road flares, and even a small tool kit with a hammer, several screwdrivers, a crescent wrench, and a pair of pliers. And best of all, two unopened rolls of duct tape.

"He wanted me to carry a gun, too," Shelly said, as Wayne organized everything. "But that's where I drew the line. Guess I should've listened to him, huh."

She didn't have a backpack, but Wayne was able to improvise her work bag. Shelly was fine with leaving her tape recorder behind, but she insisted on keeping the tape of her interview with Old Bob, and a pair of notebooks: one with the notes from that interview, and a blank one she intended to fill with quotes and observations along the way.

"Well, I guess that's everything." Wayne grabbed the hatch door to shut it.

Craig stuck his head in the car. "Hold up, there's one

more thing I want to get." He searched for a moment, then pulled out the tire iron. "This would've been helpful the other night." He hefted it in one hand and smacked the palm of his other, testing its weight.

"Good thinking," Wayne said. He was glad to see Craig contributing to the group more. Wayne didn't know if he was doing it to impress Shelly or protect her, and he didn't care one way or the other. It was nice to have everyone on the same page for once. Craig might have been okay with arguing, but Wayne wasn't. He'd never been comfortable with confrontation, but since they'd made him their de facto leader, he didn't have much choice. And while he didn't want the role, he knew it made sense. He'd been here the longest, and he was the oldest. He also had more experience in the outdoors than they did. Erik said he and Koko used to go camping in the summer, but Craig was pretty green. Fortunately, he was a quick learner. Wayne taught him how to use the flint-striker to start a fire, since the lighters Erik had found wouldn't last forever, and how to skin, clean, and cook the squixels.

Shelly had no problem prepping them for the fire, either. "I grew up on a farm," she'd explained as she removed the organs from a large male squixel. "I could neuter the little buggers for you if you want me to."

Erik laughed at that. "You better watch yourself, Craig. Sounds like she has plans for you."

Wayne was surprised to see Craig blush. Shelly was turning out to be just what their little family needed. And that's exactly how he was starting to think of their group. A family. They hadn't known each other long, but they'd gone through a lot of shit together in a very short time.

All in all, he was feeling good about their chances.

"Well, kids, I think we should have one last night here, and tomorrow we'll head out. What do you think?"

Everyone nodded in agreement, including Sammie and Koko.

"Great, then it's settled. We'll throw a few more squixels on the barbie tonight—"

"On the barbie?" Shelly side-eyed Wayne.

Craig leaned in. "*Crocodile Dundee*. I'll tell you later."

"Yes, on the barbie," Wayne continued, grinning. "And tomorrow morning, we'll head off."

"Which way do you want to go?" Erik asked.

"Let's wait and see which direction the sun rises."

Shelly leaned over to Craig. "Which direction the sun rises? Is he kidding?"

"It's complicated," Craig said. "I'll tell you about that later, too." He put his arm around her shoulder, and she leaned into him.

Wayne caught Sammie's eye and winked. Sammie winked back.

# CHAPTER TWENTY

"I told you they tasted like chicken," Craig told Shelly.

Shelly licked her fingers. "Yeah, but you didn't tell me it was hotel banquet chicken!"

Wayne laughed. "I can't believe your dad didn't pack some salt and pepper with your survival gear for protection against bland taste."

"I always seemed to have some extra ketchup packs floating around in my glove box," Erik said. "Lotta good that does us now, though."

Craig threw some meat to the dogs. "Koko and Sammie don't mind my cooking," he said.

"I don't know about Sammie, but Koko also likes to eat cat shit," Erik said. "I call 'em Zagnuts."

"Nobody said it was bad." Shelly held up a piece and stared at it. "Just bland. So, so bland. I bet you put raisins in your potato salad."

Craig feigned indignation. "Who doesn't?"

"Um, people with good taste?" Shelly handed him her bones.

Craig stood and gathered the rest of the waste. "On that

note, I'm gonna go bury these so the dogs don't choke on them." He tripped over the tire iron and leaned it against his seat before walking off to the side of the station. That's when he noticed a man standing just out of the firelight.

He turned around and hurried back to the fire. "Hey, guys, I forgot something," he said, louder than he needed to.

Wayne cocked his head in confusion.

Craig lowered his voice to just above a whisper. "There's a man standing at the edge of the parking lot. I don't know how long he's been there."

Shelly gasped. "What? How did the dogs not notice him?"

"Those things in the woods were able to sneak up on us, too," Erik said. "I don't know how, but they did."

Before they had even decided what to do, the man had made his way into their camp. The dogs both stood up, growling and baring their teeth—

"Can we help you?"

The man snapped his head in Wayne's direction, as though his words had brought him out of a trance. "Huh? I'm sorry. My brain's a little funky." He twirled his finger in a circle near his temple. "Ain't been around people in forever, seems like." He licked his lips. "Ain't eaten nothing in forever, either. I could smell you from miles away."

"Wait, did you say you could smell *us* from miles away?" Craig asked, already suspicious of the visitor.

"What? No, why would I say that? I meant I could smell whatever it is you're cooking."

"The squixels?" Wayne asked. "I'm sorry, but we just ate the last of them. Maybe one of the dogs could catch you one, but they might not have much luck in the dark."

"Don't worry about it," the man said. "Can I just sit

with you by the fire? Like I said, it's been forever since I been around any people. I'll figure out something to eat in a bit."

It wasn't until Craig could see his features in the firelight that he realized how emaciated the man was. Sunken cheeks, thin skin stretched tight across his skull. Most troubling to Craig, though, were his sunglasses. They instantly brought back memories of the night Vaughn had abandoned him on the roadside, and the way he'd worn sunglasses to hide his orange eyes.

"Hey, sorry, man, but we were all about to pack it in for the night." Craig stood up and motioned for the others to follow him. "We're all sleeping in the station. You're welcome to sleep out here if you'd like."

Wayne didn't move. "What's your hurry, Craig? He's the first person we've seen in a while, too."

"Yeah, Craig, where are your manners? I'm glad you didn't treat me like this." Shelly tugged on his arm, pulling him down next to her.

Erik had finally gotten Sammie and Koko to stop growling, but they shared Craig's apprehension. Why wasn't anyone else picking up on that?

"I'm Wayne, this is Erik, Shelly, and Craig. What's your name?"

The man cocked his head. "My name? Dang, that's a good question. I honestly can't remember," he said. "I've been wandering in the darkness for so long it musta slipped my mind."

"Wandering in the darkness? What does that even mean?" Craig snapped. "The sun just set a few hours ago."

"That's another good question," the man answered. "I was somewhere dark for like, forever. And then a door opened, and I was somewhere not-dark." He swept his arm to the sky. "This ain't dark. It's still so damn bright."

"Is that why you're wearing sunglasses... at night?" Craig nearly spat the words. No way was he letting a stranger get the better of him again.

The man ignored his question. "I'm looking for a place. Don't remember where I heard about it, but supposedly it's a... what's the word?" He paused. "Next... nexist... no, *nexus*! That's it. I'm looking for a nexus between worlds. It's supposed to be in the middle of a field, surrounded by rows of plants taller than your head. If you can find your way through to the center, you can find your way anywhere. But it's a lot harder than it sounds. Some huge creature guards it. Most of the people who try don't make it. Either the monster gets 'em, or one of the things that walk behind the rows does."

Shelly dropped Craig's hand. "Holy crap, that sounds like a corn maze! I was just at one." She looked at the others. "Old Bob, the man I interviewed before I found you? He owns and operates the county's oldest maze. A few people have disappeared in it over the years. More important for us, though, he said people have also *appeared* in it, too. Just showed up in the maze, seemingly out of thin air."

Erik perked up. "Wait, you don't think it's the same place, do you?"

"I don't know, but it sounds too similar to be a coincidence, doesn't it?" Shelly asked.

"Shelly's right," Wayne said. "I guess we know where we're going tomorrow morning. We'll head back down the road in the direction she came from."

Craig couldn't believe what he was hearing. Hadn't they learned anything from what he'd told them about Vaughn?

"Hold up. You're gonna believe some guy we just met, what, ten minutes ago? Has everyone gone crazy but me?"

Shelly touched his arm. "No, I think it makes sense. It matches Old Bob's story."

Craig yanked his arm away and stood up. He spun and jabbed his finger at the stranger. "Why the fuck are you wearing shades? Does the name Vaughn mean anything to you?" He reached for the man's face. "Let me see your eyes! Take those off now, or I'll take them off for you!"

Sammie and Koko growled again. Craig wasn't sure if it was aimed at him or the stranger. Right now, he didn't care.

The man stepped back out of Craig's reach. "Sorry, dude. I understand. I'll take 'em off. No problem." He reached up and slowly removed the glasses. "See?"

Craig braced himself, ready to attack if the man's eyes were orange. But they weren't. They were blue. Very, very blue. And his nails were exceptionally long, like talons. He'd kept his hands folded in his lap until this point.

Suddenly it all clicked into place. The darkness, the door, the eyes, the nails. "Erik, he's a bat. Like from the hotel!"

The man lurched forward and reached for Shelly. He was fast; the dogs were faster. Sammie went for his legs, Koko launched herself at his face. He kicked Sammie to the side. Koko he caught in mid-air and threw her into the fire, then spun and advanced toward Shelly.

This time Erik jumped at him, forcing him to step back. Craig grabbed the tire iron and swung at his head while Wayne closed in from the other side. Together, they pushed him back another step. Then another. Sammie went for his legs again and he fell backward in slow motion, waving his arms in circles trying to catch his balance, before falling onto their wood pile. A sharp branch burst through his chest.

The man threw his head back and howled. His body smoked, then erupted into white flames so bright everyone had to turn their heads. When they could look again, all that was left was a pile of smoldering ashes.

Erik ran back to the fire to find that Koko had dragged herself out of the flames. Her fur had burned away, and blisters covered her skin, but she was alive. Before his eyes, the blisters healed themselves and her fur grew back. It happened so fast he didn't have a chance to tell the others.

"Holy shit, guys!" Shelly exclaimed. "Was that an actual vampire?"

"If it was, he's the stupidest fucking vampire ever," Craig smirked. "Why didn't he just turn into a bat? Dumbass."

Sammie squatted and peed on his ashes.

# CHAPTER TWENTY-ONE

Wayne decided they needed to set a watch for the rest of the night and volunteered to take the first shift. He and Sammy were sitting by the window, watching the parking lot, when Erik joined them. Soft moonlight illuminated the front of the store.

"Couldn't sleep?" Wayne patted the floor next to him.

"Nope." Erik sat down and leaned against a display case. "Koko's out, though. So are Craig and Shelly."

"How is Koko?"

"Fine. She's snoring away and her paws are kicking up a storm, but that's normal for her."

Wayne sighed. "I don't even know what to say at this point. Whatever that reaper did to her, she seems pretty much indestructible."

Erik shook his head. "Her fur had burned away, her skin had blisters all over it, and they just...disappeared. She healed herself right in front of me. It happened so fast, too."

"I told you how Sammie seems younger since we crossed over," Wayne said, "but it's nothing like that. A few months back, before we ran into you all, I had to pull a big splinter from one of her pads. She winced and yelped like a little baby." He reached over and rubbed Sammie's neck. "And it certainly didn't heal on its own right away."

"Koko's lucky, I guess."

"You both are," Wayne said. "And we're lucky to have met you."

"Same. I can't imagine being out here on our own. I'm sure Koko would be fine, but I'd probably be dead by now."

"So, you didn't get any of those healing powers, huh?"

Erik laughed. "Hardly." He showed Wayne his left hand, which had a row of blisters across the palm. "Got those putting out the fire on Koko's fur." Next, he pulled up his shirt so Wayne could see the large bruise on his ribs. "Got this when we were running from those things in the woods. Couple more on my legs, too."

The two men sat in silence for a few minutes, looking out the window and taking turns petting Sammie. Finally, Wayne stretched and yawned. "Well, if you really can't sleep, I think I'm gonna try to catch a few zees, if that's okay with you."

Erik nodded. "Fine by me." He tilted his chin toward the parking lot. "For what it's worth, I think we'll be okay. Only two bats escaped that room before we got the door shut, and now both of them are dead."

"I hope you're right." Wayne stood up. He didn't want to consider the possibility that there might be more of them out there. "You coming, Sammie?" She thumped her tail but made no effort to get up.

"Guess she's staying here," Erik said.

Wayne paused at the *Employees Only* door. "So, we really just killed a vampire?" He shook his head in disbelief.

"Technically, I think he killed himself." Erik laughed. "But yeah, that was definitely a vampire."

"Fuck a duck."

———————

When Wayne woke up the next morning, Craig and Shelly were still sleeping. Erik must have handled the watch by himself, so Wayne decided he'd give them a little longer. He wanted to talk to Erik alone.

At the front of the store, Erik had propped the door open and was outside playing fetch with the dogs. He threw a stick for Koko, then one for Sammie. The dogs ran out to get them and raced back. Sammie's longer legs let her cover more ground, but Koko made up for it with her quickness.

Wayne watched them play for a few minutes before joining them outside. Sammie ran over to greet him, and dropped her stick at his feet.

Wayne's back cracked when he bent to pick it up. He threw it and stretched his shoulders while he waited for her to bring it back again.

Erik laughed. "I'd ask how you slept, but I think your back just gave it away."

"Yeah, getting old sucks. Wish this place made me younger and smarter like it did for the dogs."

He threw the stick again, then ambled over to where Erik was leaning against one of the old gas pumps. "Why didn't you wake up Craig or Shelly?" he asked. "It was their turn."

"I wasn't sleepy," Erik said. "No sense waking them up if I'm just gonna lie there awake, too." He pointed to the sun. "Besides, I think it's playing tricks on us again. It wasn't all that long after you went to bed that the sun came up. From the same place it set, too. The night certainly felt a lot shorter than it should have."

Wayne chuckled. "The more things change, the more they stay the same, I guess."

Koko had grown bored playing fetch and lay down at Erik's feet, while Sammie showed no signs of slowing. Wayne threw the stick a little farther for her this time. Sammie bolted after it and brought it right back. She dropped it and looked up at Wayne, her tail spinning in big circles.

"Okay, girl, one more, then we're gonna wake up Craig and Shelly and get back on the road. Whadaya say?"

Sammie spun and barked.

"This one's going deep. Ready?" He reared back and threw the stick as far as he could. It flipped end over end as it went, and disappeared before it hit the ground.

He turned to Erik. "Did you see that?"

Erik shaded his eyes. "Yeah, it looked like it just vanished in mid-air."

Sammie was running around looking for the stick. Wayne whistled for her to come back. He turned to Erik. "Let me have another."

Erik tossed a small branch over.

"I'm gonna throw it again at the same spot," Wayne said. "Let's try to watch where it goes. Maybe we just missed it last time." He told both dogs to stay. "Ready?"

Erik nodded.

This time, Wayne aimed a little higher to make it easier for them to track. This, too, flipped end over end in a nice steady arc until, once again, it disappeared in mid-air.

Wayne turned to Erik. "Holy—"

"—shit!" Shelly finished. She and Craig had just walked out of the station.

Wayne bowed. "And for my next trick, watch me pull a

rabbit out of this hat!" Craig and Erik looked at each other and shrugged.

Shelly giggled. "I love Rocky and Bullwinkle!"

"See, she gets it," Wayne said.

Craig tapped her on the shoulder. "Rocky the boxer?"

She shook her head. "No, silly, Rocky the moose."

Wayne walked up to the spot where the sticks had disappeared, giving it a wide berth. He picked up another stick and held it out in front of him until the end of it disappeared into the portal. He walked to the left, holding the stick steady, until the end reappeared. He told Erik to set a rock about a foot to the left of that spot. Then he walked back to the right. The end of the stick disappeared again. He kept walking until it reappeared. He had Erik put another rock down about a foot from that spot. He threw the stick away, then picked up more rocks and started marking a circle around the area.

"What the hell is going on?" Erik asked as he helped Wayne set more stones down.

"I've seen this before," Wayne said, hands on hips. "Or something similar, at least. It's how Sammie and I crossed over."

Craig and Shelly joined them. "So you're saying this will take us back to where you're from?" Craig asked.

"Back to 2020?" Shelly asked, apprehension in her voice.

"I don't know," Wayne admitted. He didn't want to get their hopes up. "This isn't the entry point we used, so I doubt it will take us back exactly to where we started." He tossed a rock into the portal and watched it disappear. "But it will take us somewhere. We just need to find out where."

"But didn't you say you couldn't come back through?"

Erik frowned. "That it closed behind you? That sounds like a one-way trip. What if it goes somewhere worse?"

"I thought we'd decided to look for the corn maze anyway," Craig said. "We're retracing Shelly's route."

"When we came through the first time, it was a one-way trip," Wayne confirmed. "But now we have a rope. As long as someone stays on this side, you should be able to pull them back through. You saw how that worked with the stick I was holding." He turned to Craig. "And yes, I still want to see if we can find Shelly's corn maze. But there are no guarantees it's going to be there. We all know how quickly things can change. That's why I think it's important to explore this while it's here. We're damn lucky to have found it in the first place. We owe it to ourselves to see where it goes."

Nobody said anything for a moment until finally, Erik spoke up. "I think he's right. We should check this out. If it doesn't go anywhere promising, we'll look for the corn maze."

"But what if whoever goes through can't come back?" Shelly asked. "Do we really think a piece of rope will hold it open? What if it doesn't? What if there's something dangerous on the other side, like another vampire?" She locked eyes with Erik. "Or more of those creatures from the woods?" She turned to Craig next. "Or the beast?"

"You're right," Craig said. "That's why we should send Koko through."

Erik shook his head, clearly angered by Craig's suggestion. "Whoa, hold on. No way am I sending her through there."

"Why not? She can't die, man. If there's anything dangerous, she's the best one to handle it."

"But she can't tell us what's over there," Wayne said. He

hated taking Erik's side against Craig again, but Erik was right. "Koko's smart, and maybe immortal, but last time I checked, she still can't talk."

"She doesn't need to," Craig said. "We'll fasten my phone to her collar, and she can record it. We'll let her walk around for a few minutes, then pull her back through."

"No, I won't do that to her," Erik said. "We don't know how dying and coming back affects her. I'm not taking that chance."

Wayne nodded in agreement. "And there's no way I'm letting you turn that phone on. Especially near something like this."

"Then why'd you keep it?" Craig demanded. "Why not throw it away if you don't plan on using it?"

"I don't know. But we're not turning it on. Not here. With any luck, the battery's dead anyway."

Craig threw up his arms in exasperation. "Fine. Anyone got any better ideas? I'm all ears."

"I'll go," Wayne said. "I've already been through one of these portals. It's a bit uncomfortable, but nothing too bad. And I know what to expect. Any objections?" He looked at each of them in succession. Shelly dropped her eyes. Erik shook his head.

"Fine; whatever, man," Craig said. "I still think you're making a mistake, but it's your life."

Wayne smiled. "What, no movie quote this time?"

"Nope."

"That's okay. I have one." Wayne smiled. "I'll be back."

# CHAPTER TWENTY-TWO

C raig helped Wayne tie the rope around his waist, giving the knot a good tug to make sure it wouldn't come loose. "What do you think we should do with our end of the rope?" he asked.

"What do you mean?"

"Should we tie it to something, or do you want us just to hold onto it?"

Wayne thought for a second. "That's a good point. We only have a hundred feet of rope, so it's not like I can go very far. But that doesn't give us enough slack to fasten it to one of the posts near the pumps."

"What about my car?" Shelly asked. "We should be able to roll it right up to the entrance."

Craig looked from the ring of rocks to Shelly's car, which was on the far side of the station. "That could work. I'm gonna guess it's fifty, sixty yards to here, give or take. Ground's flat, so at least we don't have to push it uphill."

Wayne gathered the rope in a loop and strung it over his shoulder. "Okay, let's do it."

Fifteen minutes later, the car was parked in front of the

portal. Craig crawled under the car and tied the rope to the front axle. He climbed out and turned to Shelly. "You're sure it's in park, right?"

Shelly rolled her eyes. "Yes, Craig, I'm sure."

"And the emergency brake is on?"

She put her hands on her hips. "Really?"

"I'm sorry," he said. "I just want to make sure we've got everything covered. We can't afford for anything to go wrong."

"I know," she said. "It won't."

Wayne patted Craig's shoulder. "Thanks for looking out for me," he said. "Even though I know you don't think I should be doing this."

"You're right, I don't."

"But you know I wouldn't be doing it if I didn't think it was worth the risk, right?"

Craig nodded, then checked the knot around Wayne's waist again.

Wayne turned to Shelly. "If anything happens, you take care of this guy, okay?"

She nodded. "You're sure about this?"

"Yeah."

"Then so am I." She pulled him in for a hug.

Finally, he turned to Erik. "I'm gonna need you to make sure Sammie doesn't follow me through." Erik nodded. He'd reattached both dogs' leashes and was holding them tight. "And if something goes wrong, you've got to take care of her for me."

He bent down and kissed Sammie on the forehead. "I'll be right back, girl. Erik's in charge while I'm gone, so you do what he says, okay?" Sammie jumped up and put her front legs around Wayne's neck. He hugged her back. "I love you, too," he said. He held her tight for another moment, then gently set her legs back on the ground. He reached over and rubbed Koko's head, then turned to the portal.

Craig followed him to the edge of the stone circle. "What do you think is going to happen?"

"Hard to say," Wayne said. "The last time it felt like I was going through a membrane of sorts. My ears popped, and then I was through. Hopefully, it'll go like that."

He took a deep breath and entered the portal.

As Craig watched, Wayne's body became two-dimensional. It stretched farther into the portal, resembling a spaceship entering hyperspace. The effect lasted a couple of seconds, and then he was gone. The rope looked like it was being pulled across the ground by something invisible, spooling out and disappearing.

"What do you think's happening over there?" Shelly asked.

Erik shrugged. Sammie and Koko were both lying at his feet, but he still held onto their leashes, just in case.

"Nothing bad, I hope," Craig said.

The rope stopped moving.

"Maybe he found something interesting." Craig picked up the rope and started spooling it out. "There's only about fifteen feet or so left, so he'll probably be coming back through soon."

No sooner had the words left his mouth than the rope pulled taut, yanking him forward. "Fuck!" He dropped it and held his hands up, rope burns slashed into both palms. Fortunately, the axle held.

Erik and Shelly both grabbed the rope and pulled. Craig joined them.

"Let's pull him back through," he said. Together, they pulled on the rope. There was little resistance at first, but after about five feet, it pulled tight again, nearly yanking

Craig into the portal. Then it fell down and stopped moving.

Erik dropped his part of the rope. "Don't pull it!" he shouted.

"Why? He could be hurt!" Craig said.

"If it's not attached and we pull it through, the portal could close. And if that happens, we might never find him again."

Craig and Shelly dropped the rope as if it were a snake.

Erik had let go of the dogs' leashes when he'd jumped to grab the rope. They waited a moment, then both ran into the portal.

# CHAPTER TWENTY-THREE

"Sammie, Koko, stay!" Erik yelled. Neither dog listened, and he watched helplessly as they disappeared into the portal.

This time, there was no hesitation on Erik's part. He was still scared—petrified, actually—but he had to help Wayne.

"I'm going in."

"Wait, let's give them a minute or two," Craig said. "Maybe Sammie and Koko can help him back through."

"Yeah, maybe." Erik shook his head. "But Wayne didn't wait when you were in trouble," he said. He was too embarrassed to admit that *he* had, a mistake he wouldn't make again. "But just in case, you two should stay here and gather up our gear. If I need help, I'll send one of the dogs back through."

He turned and walked into the portal, calmly.

The air grew thicker, soupier. It pushed down on him, almost as if it had physical weight. His ears popped and he stumbled forward, nearly stepping onto Koko, who'd been waiting for him. She grabbed his hand in her mouth and pulled him forward.

About twenty yards ahead stood the base of an enormous cliff. It ran uninterrupted in both directions as far as he could see; the top of it disappeared into low-hanging clouds. Broken rocks and scrub brush lined the bottom. Erik looked back toward where the portal should have been and saw a forest of pine that stretched off into the horizon.

"Wayne!" he yelled. "Where are you?"

"On the other side of the little tunnel," Wayne said from somewhere nearby. "Follow the rope. Koko will show you."

The rope led through a thin slit in the cliff. From this side, Erik could see treetops and mountains in the distance. That must have been what had drawn Wayne's attention. Sammie sat waiting on the other side. He was able to walk through it upright but imagined Wayne had had to duck a bit.

Wayne was sitting down, his back against this side of the cliff. He looked up at Erik, then turned away, clearly embarrassed.

"Are you okay?" Erik asked.

"I'm fine. Mostly. I twisted my ankle pretty good, though."

"What happened?"

"I walked around the other side for a few minutes, as far as the rope would let me. Then I came up to this opening and could see trees and mountaintops. Looked like it could be Colorado, so I came through to check it out. Wasn't paying attention and tripped. Nearly went over the side."

Erik walked to the edge of the corniche, looked down into the valley below, then let out a low whistle. He turned back to Wayne. "Is that...?"

"A brontosaurus? I think so."

"Holy shit. So I'm guessing this isn't Colorado."

"It could be. But it's not *our* Colorado." Wayne picked up a rock and chucked it over the cliff. "I keep waiting for a Sleestak to show up."

Erik shrugged his shoulders at Wayne's reference.

"Never mind," Wayne laughed. "Shelly would get it."

"Let's take a look at your ankle." Erik bent down and untied Wayne's boot. "Think I can take this off?"

"Do I have a choice?"

"You always have a choice, Wayne."

"I'm glad you chose to come after me," Wayne said. "Go ahead. I can handle it."

Erik pulled the boot off. Wayne moaned through gritted teeth, which made Sammie and Koko nervous. They both came and sat next to him and Sammie laid her head in his lap.

"I'm okay, girl." Wayne rubbed her neck.

"I'm gonna pull your sock off now."

"Okay."

Wayne winced but didn't cry out this time, even though his ankle had already turned an ugly shade of purple.

"I don't know if we'll get your boot back on for a while," Erik said. "Maybe I shouldn't have taken it off. Do you think you can put any weight on it?"

"Not right now, but if we can build a crutch of some sort, I'll be okay. It doesn't feel like I've broken anything, but I can't walk on it."

Erik stuffed the sock in Wayne's boot, then handed it to Koko. "Here, make yourself useful." She took the boot in her mouth and trotted off through the tunnel as he helped Wayne up.

"You ready?" Erik asked. "It might be a little awkward in the tunnel, but we should be good after that."

"Whatever you say, boss," Wayne said, wrapping an arm around Erik's neck for support. "You're in charge now."

"Don't even start that shit with me," Erik said. "Let's just take things one step at a time."

Wayne laughed. "I see what you did there."

The two men limped through the opening, Sammie on their heels. Koko was waiting at the portal entrance.

Erik walked Wayne over to a large rock and helped him to sit. "Looks like we'll try to find Shelly's maze after all," he said.

A distorted voice broke the silence.

"*Errrriik...*"

It was Craig, but it sounded as if he were yelling through a long metal pipe. Erik turned in time to see him stumble out of the portal.

"Over here," Erik said.

Craig ran to where they were sitting. "Thank you, sweet Baby Jesus! You two are okay," he said, trying to catch his breath. "You've been gone a while. We were getting worried."

"It hasn't been that long. Not over here, at least." Wayne pointed to his foot. "Just twisted my ankle. I'll be fine once we make a crutch."

"So, what do you think? Should I get Shelly and our gear?" Craig was checking out the landscape as he spoke.

Erik shook his head. "Nope, this isn't home. We're gonna go back and find Shelly's maze."

"What makes you so certain?" Craig asked. He inspected the vegetation along the base of the cliff. "Looks like it could be Colorado to me."

Erik pointed to the sky, where a pterodactyl soared overhead. "That."

# CHAPTER TWENTY-FOUR

"What took you so long?" Shelly ran to Craig, who was on his way out of the portal. "I was about to come in after you."

Craig waved her off. "Everything's fine. Well, we did see a fucking pterodactyl."

"And a brontosaurus," Erik added.

Shelly's jaw dropped.

"I know, right?" Craig smiled. "Other than that, it was no big deal. I literally went in, grabbed these two, and came back out. You know how tricky time can be here."

"That's why I waited as long as I did. But it doesn't mean I'm not allowed to worry."

"Waiting was the right call," Wayne said. Shelly watched as Erik helped him sit down on the bumper of her car.

"What happened? Are you okay?" Shelly grabbed the first aid kit from their gear.

"I'm fine," he said. "Just twisted my ankle a little."

Shelly took a closer look. "A little? I'm no doctor, but that looks like a serious sprain." Wayne winced as she felt the swelling. "Sorry," she said. "I don't think it's broken, but like I said—"

"You're no doctor," Wayne finished for her. "I think I'd know if I'd broken it. I just need you to help me wrap it up good and tight. Craig or Erik can make me a crutch, and we can get back on the road."

"Are you crazy? You need to keep off that foot for at least a day or two, if not longer." She turned to Craig and Erik. "Guys, back me up here."

Erik nodded. "She's right, Wayne. There's no reason for us to leave right now anyway. We can wait until your ankle heals up some."

Wayne turned to Craig. "What do you think?"

"Well, I hate to say I told you so, but I think if you'd have listened to me, you'd be fine. I guess we have to wait now, don't we?"

Shelly's shoulders tightened. She didn't understand Craig's attitude toward Wayne.

"Let it go, Craig," Erik said. "I told you I wasn't going to send Koko through by herself."

"And I told you we weren't turning your phone back on," Wayne added. "I guess waiting a couple days isn't that big a deal in the grand scheme of things." He looked toward the sky. "Let's hope the weather holds out and we don't get any storms. A scene-quake is the last thing we need right now."

"Whatever, man. I'll go find some wood for your crutch," Craig said over his shoulder as he stomped away from the group.

"Craig, wait!" Shelly yelled. "We might have something here in the woodpile we can use!"

"Let him go," Wayne told her. "He gets this way sometimes. He just needs to blow off some steam."

"Does this happen a lot?" Shelly asked as she watched Craig walk away. This was a new level of hostility. She didn't like it. Her ex-boyfriend Max had had a bit of a short fuse. Nothing too bad, but it was there. Everything had been going great between them until she'd been offered the job at the newspaper. That meant she'd have to move.

Max had been supportive at first. He'd even offered to move with her. She didn't think it was fair for him to uproot his life, especially since he still had three more quarters until he graduated, so she'd said no. She'd thought they could try a long-distance relationship, but Max hadn't liked that idea. In what felt to her like a last-ditch effort, he proposed. And while she'd certainly considered it, she realized she wasn't ready. She wanted to follow her career. So she'd turned him down. He didn't take her refusal well, and his temper boiled over. They'd ended on bad terms. She'd felt terrible, but if she were being honest with herself, she also felt relieved. It was definitely something to keep an eye on with Craig.

"Not a lot," Erik said. "I'd cut him some slack. Before you showed up, he'd told me he felt really alone. Me and Wayne have Koko and Sammie. He didn't have anybody. And the way he ended up over here was a lot harder on him than it was us." He smiled. "Besides, I think you're good for him."

"I hope so."

"You're good for each other," Wayne chimed in. "It's rough out here. It helps to have someone you can lean on when you need to."

Shelly nodded. She was uncomfortable with the focus on her, so she changed the subject. "Okay, let's get that ankle wrapped up," she said. "Then we'll get you back to the shelter." She snapped her fingers at the dogs. "Sammie,

Koko, go rustle us up some dinner." They ran off together, happy to be hunting again.

When she was done, Erik helped Wayne over to the station. Shelly was impressed with how Wayne had handled the pain as she'd wrapped his ankle. He wasn't nearly as big a baby as most of the men she knew. Smiling to herself, she picked up Wayne's pack and carried it over for him.

By the time Craig made it back from the woods, she'd skinned and skewered the ten squixels the dogs had caught.

"Hey guys, I'm sorry about earlier," he said sheepishly. "I was just upset about Wayne getting hurt."

Wayne waved him off. "I'm not the one you need to apologize to."

"Yeah, I know."

Craig turned to Shelly. "Can we talk? Over there, maybe?"

Shelly nodded and followed him to her car. When they stopped, she asked, "Why did you get so upset?"

"Look, I love Wayne," Craig said, clearly struggling to explain his feelings, "but he doesn't listen to me and treats me like I'm a kid half the time. Sure, he's probably saved my life more than once, but still, I'm a grown-ass man."

Shelly gave him a puzzled look.

"It's an expression," he said. "It means I'm an adult and deserve to be treated with respect. Like that whole bit about the phone. It's my goddamned phone, not his. But he took it like he's my dad."

"But didn't he say it caused scape-quakes?"

"Scene-quakes," Craig corrected her. "And yeah, that's what he says, but he doesn't know if it's true or not. And if he has any proof, he hasn't shared it with us. We're just supposed to take him at his word."

"Why wouldn't we? Has he ever lied to you before?"

Craig shrugged. "Yes? No? Maybe? I don't know. That's the problem. If he'd listened to me and used the phone to record the other side of the portal, he never would've gotten hurt. And we wouldn't be stuck here waiting for his ankle to get better instead of looking for the maze."

"I still don't know if I believe you about that thing," Shelly said. "It's small enough to fit in your pocket, but you can make movies with it?"

"Record videos, but yeah. You can record conversations with it, too. You'd love it. It'd make your job a lot easier. It's connected to this thing called the world wide web, or the internet, that lets you look up anything instantaneously. It's like having access to the world's biggest research library whenever you want. It has real-time maps and directions called GPS, Global Positioning System. You can't get lost with it."

"That would be nice," Shelly said. "Of course, then I'd have never met you."

Craig dropped his gaze. "Uhm, you can also read books on it and watch movies," he said. "And talk to anyone pretty much anywhere in the world. It's like the world's biggest computer, but it's barely bigger than a deck of cards."

"Now I know you're pulling my leg. Movie cameras are huge. Tape recorders are pretty big, too. Computers can take up entire floors of a building. And this inter...net thing is what, just floating around in the air?" Shelly had considered asking Wayne or Erik about the phone, but knew it would just cause an argument.

"Basically. I wish I could show it to you, but the internet doesn't work over here, obviously. Besides, Wayne has it in his pack."

"Oh, he does, does he?" Shelly pulled out Craig's phone.

She'd nicked it from Wayne's pack when she'd carried it over to the station earlier.

Craig's eyes widened. "How'd you get that?"

"Just something I picked up in the pokey." Shelly grinned and batted her eyes.

"What?"

"Kidding. Sometimes reporters have to be a little sneaky to get the story."

"Put it away for now," Craig said, glancing over his shoulder to make sure Wayne wasn't looking. "Later tonight I'll show you what it does, after they go to sleep."

"Well, I would like to see what all the fuss is about."

She let her fingers brush his when they walked back to the station. She didn't have to look to know that he was blushing.

# CHAPTER TWENTY-FIVE

Craig said he and Shelly would take the last watch. Erik didn't think they needed to keep watch, but Wayne said he'd feel better if they did. Especially since he couldn't jump up and run around with his bad ankle. Better safe than sorry, he said.

They waited until they were sure Erik and Wayne were both asleep, then snuck outside the station. Koko looked up at them from her place near the door but didn't bother getting up. When they reached the side of the building, Shelly pulled the phone out of her bag and handed it to Craig. "Are you sure about this?" she asked.

"Of course," he lied. In truth, he was only about ninety percent sure, but he was willing to risk the other ten percent in order to impress her. He'd show her something quick and easy, just in case Wayne was right. Besides, he was really hoping he'd be able to talk her into going back to his time instead of the '70s, so he needed all the help he could get. He wasn't sure his personality was enough to pull that off, especially the way he'd lashed out at Wayne.

He could tell his outburst had upset her. He was counting on the phone to be his secret weapon.

That was assuming they could even get back to his world, of course. He still didn't trust what that vampire had told them, and couldn't understand why everyone else did. That didn't mean they shouldn't at least check it out, though. Especially if it made Shelly happy.

"Fingers crossed the battery's not dead," he said as he powered it up. "I'm gonna look like a total idiot if it won't even turn on."

Shelly laughed. "You could never look like a total idiot to me." She gave him a quick peck on the cheek. "A half-idiot? Sure. But total? Never."

Craig was glad it was night, so she couldn't see his face turn red. His heart was beating so loud, though, he was worried she might hear it.

"My word, Craig, I can't be certain under the moonlight, since there's only one out tonight, but I do believe you might be blushing."

*Damn it!*

"I just really like hanging out together," he said, hoping his voice wasn't too shaky.

"Is that what we're doing? Hanging out?" Shelly leaned back. "I was hoping maybe we could try *making* out."

Craig couldn't believe his luck. He'd been hoping for this, but he'd been afraid to make a move. Not only because he didn't want to upset the group dynamic, but also because, despite his outbursts, he was actually pretty shy. Instead, he'd been playing it safe with what he thought was harmless flirting. It was almost as if he'd been trying to put himself in the friend zone. But no, she was really interested. In him! He was leaning in to kiss her when his phone booted up.

*DING DING DING!* The opening notes sounded entirely too loud out here under the alien sky. He covered the speakers with his hand and shielded the screen. But it was too late. The moment was gone.

"What in the..." Shelly's jaw dropped. All thoughts of making out had clearly vanished. "You were telling the truth. Look at it!"

"That's just the sign-on screen," Craig said. "But yeah, I was telling the truth." He checked the battery meter. It showed less than ten percent left. He was actually thankful Wayne had turned it off when he'd taken it from him. It would've been dead for sure, otherwise.

Shelly reached for it. "So come on, show it to me!" Craig held it just out of reach, forcing her to lean across him. She put her hand on his thigh for balance and tried to pull his arm down. "Give it to me!"

"Okay, okay." Craig acted like he was going to hand her the phone, then pulled it back at the last second. "On one condition."

"Name it."

"Gimme some sugar, baby," he said with a smile.

"What?"

"Sorry, I meant—"

She cut him off with a full-on kiss. His body stiffened. She pulled back. "Are you... did you not want me to...?"

"No, of course I wanted you to," he said. "I just wasn't sure if you wanted to."

"How much more obvious could I make it?"

This time, he didn't have to lean in for the kiss. After a few minutes, he tentatively slipped his hand up her shirt. She didn't stop him. When she rubbed his groin, he jumped up. "Come on, let's get in the car," he said. "The last thing I want is for Wayne and Erik to see my bare ass in the moonlight."

"That's pretty presumptuous on your part," Shelly said.

"What? Oh my god, I'm so sorry. I'm such an idiot! This is so embarrassing." He pulled away and rubbed his hands over his face. "What was I thinking?"

"You were thinking right." Shelly grinned and grabbed his hand. "I just meant it was presumptuous to think you'd be on top."

Afterward, they lay in the backseat, wrapped around each other. "Did you feel that?" Craig asked.

"Feel what?"

"The ground. It shook."

"Well, someone's a little full of themselves," Shelly laughed.

"Ha ha. I'm being serious, though. Just wait a second."

The crucifix hanging from her rearview mirror swayed.

"You had to have felt that, right?"

Shelly sat up. "Yeah, I did." She wriggled back into her shirt. "You don't think...?"

As Craig threw his pants on, his phone fell out of his pocket. The screen was still lit up.

The ground shook again. Harder this time.

Craig jumped out of the car. In the distance, a new mountain had appeared. But he knew it wasn't a mountain.

His heart dropped.

The beast was back.

# CHAPTER TWENTY-SIX

The sound of barking yanked Wayne from his sleep. Erik, Craig, and Shelly were gathering their gear as quickly as they could. Lightning flashes illuminated the parking lot and bled into the station.

Erik handed Wayne his crutch. "Come on, we have to go. I'll take your pack, but I need you to get ready. It's not safe to stay here."

Wayne pushed himself up into a seated position. "What's going on?"

"The beast is back," Shelly said. She wouldn't meet his eyes.

Wayne opened his pack and saw the phone was gone.

"Jesus Christ, Craig, you turned your phone on, didn't you?"

"It's not his fault," Shelly said. "I asked him to do it. I'm the one who took it from your pack."

"But why?" Wayne was up and limping toward the front door.

"It doesn't matter," Craig said. "I'm the one who turned it on. I'm to blame for this, not Shelly."

"But we can just stay here in the station," Wayne said. "They're immune to scene-quakes."

"Not this one," Erik said. "The pumps out front have disappeared and reappeared twice. And the back half of the store fuzzed and faded, like static on a TV."

"But how?" Wayne was having a hard time digesting this change of events. It put everything he thought he knew about the Far Beyond into question.

"Does it matter?" Craig snapped. "We can't stay here. It's not safe."

"What are we supposed to do, then? Outrun it?"

"I did," Craig said.

"Yeah, but you weren't on crutches!" Wayne yelled. How had he let that happen?

Craig grabbed him by the shoulders. "Look, I'm sorry about this, okay? When we're safe again, you can yell at me, kick my ass; hell, you can banish me if it'll make you feel better, I don't care. I deserve it. But right now, we have to move. Besides, I don't think we need to outrun it. We just need to outlast the storm. I think that's how we got away last time."

"I think he's right," Erik said. "At least about the needing to move part. We'll take our chances with the beast. But if we wait here, I'm pretty sure it's gonna stomp us to death."

Wayne turned to Shelly. "What do you think?"

"I'm with them," she said. "I saw that thing. Granted, it was from a distance, but that was close enough for me."

"Where's your phone now, Craig?" Wayne asked, trying to keep the edge out of his voice.

"I smashed it by the car."

"Good. Maybe the beast will stop there." Wayne picked up the rope and tied one end of it around his waist. He handed it to Shelly. "I want everyone to loop this around their waist. We need to make sure we don't get separated in the scene-quake, or we'll never find each other again."

"What about the dogs?" Erik asked. "Do we have enough rope to tie them to us, too?"

"Just loop their leashes around the rope," Wayne explained. "Like this." He took Sammie's leash and looped it around the rope between he and Shelly, then pulled the end of the leash through the handle. "It will give them a little leeway and keep them from running off."

"Good idea." Erik attached Koko's leash to the section of rope between he and Craig.

Wayne checked the rope. Erik and Koko were in the lead, followed by Craig, Shelly, and Sammie. He was bringing up the rear. He didn't say it out loud, but he'd taken the last spot so he could untie himself if he thought he was slowing them down too much.

"Now remember, the landscape is going to change as we move. It'll probably happen in time with the lightning. You have to be ready for anything. You won't believe some of the things you're going to see. The trick is to keep moving. But whatever happens, don't panic."

"Fear is the mind-killer," Craig and Shelly said at the same time.

"Jinx, owe me a Coke!" Shelly giggled nervously.

"And we owe you our lives," Craig said. "If you hadn't stopped to help us—"

"Save it," Shelly interrupted. "We're gonna make it; right, Wayne?"

Wayne put on a brave face for the group. "Damn right."

When Erik opened the door, sheets of rain blew in, soaking them before they'd even got started. "You guys ready?"

Everyone nodded.

Erik led them into the storm.

# CHAPTER TWENTY-SEVEN

E rik and Craig had barely left the station when a bolt of lightning hit the canopy over the gas pumps, sending sparks raining down onto the parking lot in a shower of orange and yellow. Craig shielded his eyes, then turned back to check on Shelly.

The store flashed and froze, as though the image was buffering. Shelly, Sammie, and Wayne flickered, then disappeared.

"Shelly!" Craig screamed, and yanked the rope to get Erik's attention. Erik ran back to where Craig was standing. "What's wrong?" he yelled into Craig's ear.

"Shelly and Wayne, they're gone!" He pointed back to the station where Shelly, Sammie, and Wayne were coming out of the door. *What the hell?*

They huddled together under the store's awning. "Is everything okay?" Shelly yelled, struggling to raise her voice above the storm.

Wayne cupped his mouth and shouted. "Why'd you stop?"

Craig didn't know what to say. His previous encounter

with the beast had been scary enough, but nothing had prepared him for the hopelessness of seeing his friends blink in and out of existence. He shrugged his shoulders and gave Erik the thumbs-up to keep going.

They made it to the edge of the parking lot before the next flash transformed the landscape into a field of roses. A single beam of light illuminated a tall, dark structure that towered above them. As one, they stopped, transfixed.

Craig rubbed his neck, then lifted his eyes to the sky. He felt an ancient, malevolent presence stirring in the cosmos. Their intrusion hadn't gone unnoticed, and he understood on a primal level that if this entity were to turn its eye on them, his mind would break.

"We gotta keep moving!" He pushed Erik so hard he nearly knocked him over.

Storm clouds rolled in from the west. The entity turned in their direction and raced above the field toward them. Craig screamed and fell, fetal, gibbering under his breath as he tried to hide.

Lightning struck the tower, and they were in a prairie, surrounded by teepees arranged in a loose circle. Shelly helped Craig to his feet, and they started moving again. Another flash and they stumbled onto a metal bridge connecting two darkened castles, where burnt and tattered banners hung from the gates. A dragon circled high overhead.

The next flash transported them to a dead city. Trash blew down the street past the burnt-out shells of cars and delivery trucks. A metal sign screeched a sad song in the distance as it swayed in the acrid breeze. The moon emerged from behind a blackened skyscraper, far larger and closer than it should have been.

As the ground shook, a chain-link fence surrounding an

empty parking lot across the street rattled. The moon's reflection in the tower glass vibrated before storm clouds blocked its light. Multiple windows shattered, raining glass down onto the street. Craig didn't need to see the beast to know they hadn't escaped it yet.

Wayne yelled from his place at the back of the line. "Keep going! It's still coming!" Together they moved deeper into the city.

Another flash and they staggered into an ossuary that stretched to the horizon in every direction, choking on bone dust as they stumbled through ancient skeletons of animals, adults, and children.

The rope behind him pulled tight. Craig turned and saw that Shelly had fallen into a pile of children's skulls. He helped her up and hugged her, begging her to hang on, promising her it would all be over soon.

Next they were on a tractor path bisecting a field of grain. They kept moving as the rain washed the bone dust from their hair and clothes, until they were heading down a lonely two-lane highway. About ten yards from the side of the road, Craig saw a billboard for "Old Bob's Corn Maze Spectacular." A bolt of lightning hit the sign, and it disappeared.

"Did you see that?" Craig yelled, trying to be heard above the storm. "It was a sign for the maze! It vanished when the scenery changed."

"At least it means we're heading in the right direction," Wayne yelled. "Or we were."

"Let's keep going that way," said Erik. He turned to Shelly. "Did you see it?"

She struggled to shield her face from the rain. "No, but I believe Craig. If he said he saw it, he saw it!" She turned to Wayne. "How's your ankle? Are we going too fast?"

Wayne waved her off. "Don't worry about me," he said. "I'll keep up."

Sammie and Koko paced alongside the group, anxious to get moving again.

While they were huddled together, another bolt of lightning spider-webbed across the sky. This time, they all saw the sign for Old Bob's. The paint had faded, and it leaned far to the right. One more big gust of wind and they might have missed it.

Shelly pointed toward a cornfield in the distance. Without speaking, they started for it. A discordant howl behind them let them know the beast was still on the move, although it sounded farther away than before.

Lightning flashed again. The immediate landscape changed, but the cornfield remained the same.

"Maybe it's immune to the scene-quakes!" Wayne yelled.

*That's what we thought about the Koko stations*, Craig thought. He kept it to himself, though, since it was his fault they were running for their lives to begin with.

It took about ten minutes before they finally reached the maze, slowed down as they were by Wayne's ankle, and it was much as Shelly had described it: an old farmhouse next to a gravel parking lot, with a decaying sign advertising *Old Bob's Corn Maze Spectacular*. But this wasn't the maze from Shelly's world. The paint was peeling. Windows were broken or missing. The front screen door hung by a single hinge, and there were dozens of small holes in the siding.

Craig stepped out of the looped rope, then walked up and stuck his finger in one of them. "I think these are bullet holes."

"This isn't right," Shelly said as she dropped the rope

from around her waist. "The sign is misspelled. It should say *Maize Spooktacular*. And where is everybody? There aren't any cars or trucks anywhere."

"Whatever happened here, it couldn't have been good," Wayne said. He turned to Erik. "What's it look like behind us?"

Erik scanned the horizon. "So far, so good. I don't see it anywhere. Storm seems to be letting up, too. We probably have a few minutes to scope out the place, see if we can figure out what happened here if you want, Shelly."

Craig stood at the top of the porch steps and looked out at the maze. A darkness shimmered high above the corn, as if the night had ripped a hole through time and space. He blinked, and the sky returned to normal.

Wayne untied himself and limped to the maze entrance. "As bad as the house looks, I'm more interested in the state of the maze," he said. "There are no weeds in the dirt between the rows. The fact that there are still orderly rows is even weirder. If I had to guess, I'd say someone has been taking care of it, which can't be true, or—"

"Or it really *is* a nexus point," Erik said. He untied himself and let Sammie and Koko off their leashes. Both dogs sniffed around the outside of the maze, but neither showed any signs of wanting to go in.

As the four of them gathered together in the parking lot, a massive bolt of lightning hit the weathervane atop the farmhouse. Less than a mile away, the beast reappeared. It would be on them in a few moments.

Craig didn't hesitate. "You guys go, I have an idea," he told them. He pulled his phone out of his pack and powered it up.

"You had it the whole time?" Wayne yelled. "For fuck's

sake! No wonder it could follow us. I thought you'd left it back at the station?"

"I lied." Craig turned the phone on. "It's been turned off, but I thought I might need it." He hadn't told anyone about his plan because he knew they'd try to talk him out of it.

"Need it for what?" Shelly asked.

Craig waited a few more seconds for the screen to light up. "This." He grabbed Shelly and kissed her. "You take care of these guys, okay? I got us into this, and I'm going to get us out of it."

He turned and ran toward the beast, holding the phone high above his head like a sword.

Shelly looked at Wayne and Erik, tears in her eyes. "I'm sorry, but I can't let him do this on his own." She ran after Craig, shouting his name.

The dogs whined, torn between going after Craig and Shelly or protecting Erik and Wayne.

Shelly caught up to him seconds after he reached the beast. "You want this, motherfucker?" Craig screamed. The beast looked down at them. "Come on... Come on! Do it!"

The beast opened its mouth and emitted a beam of blue-white light which enveloped Craig and Shelly. Sparks danced on the ground and in their hair.

Craig put his arm around her. He'd meant to do this alone, to make up for all the trouble he'd caused, but having her at his side felt right. Above them, the light from the beast's mouth intensified, surpassing the brilliance of a noonday sun. Blinded, he pulled Shelly closer. Over the roar of the beast, he heard her say, "Give me some sugar, baby."

He kissed her and the world went white.

# CHAPTER TWENTY-EIGHT

The shock wave from the explosion knocked Erik and Wayne off their feet and blew over the maze sign.

After checking himself for injuries, Erik helped Wayne up and handed him his crutch. Spots dotted his vision. Where Shelly, Craig, and the beast had stood was a smoldering black scar. The rain stopped and the clouds cleared. Blue sky stretched across the horizon.

"What do you think happened to them?" Erik asked. His ears were still ringing.

"I have no idea," Wayne said. "Maybe they killed it? Maybe it killed them? Maybe they got lucky and were transported somewhere else? We'll probably never know for sure."

Sammie and Koko trotted over to the scar and sniffed around the circle. Sammie walked to the edge of the scar, where the beast had stood, and peed on it. Koko lifted her nose in the air, as if she could still catch Craig and Shelly's scents, and whined, confused about where her friends could be. She looked back at Erik and whimpered.

"I don't know where they are, girl. Hopefully someplace

better than this." He patted his leg, and she came back to his side. Sammie walked over and lay down next to Wayne's feet.

They stood in silence for a few moments, then Erik turned to Wayne. "I guess there's no point in putting it off. You ready to go?"

Wayne shook his head. "We're not going."

Erik's jaw dropped. "What do you mean you're not going? Craig and Shelly gave their lives so we could get back to our world!"

Wayne's face fell at Erik's accusation. "I know. If anyone was going to sacrifice themselves, it was supposed to be me. That's why I took the last loop in the rope. I didn't know Craig had other plans." Erik thought Wayne looked ashamed that Craig had beat him to it. "But Sammie and I were never going through that maze. I wanted to help everyone find their way back, but this is our home now."

"You can't mean that," Erik said. But he knew Wayne did.

"There's nothing for us to go back to, Erik. My life essentially ended when that drunk driver killed Lori. Chuck helped us through the worst of it, but most of the time I was just going through the motions." He bent down to pet his dog. "And Sammie was really slowing down over there. You only know her like this. I can't take a chance on her regressing if we go back." He took a deep breath. "I'm sorry, but we're staying."

"Are you sure?"

"Yes. We're happy here; right, Sammie?

Sammie jumped up with a severe case of wiggle-butt.

"Then we're staying, too." A sense of calm spread through Erik's body. He knew it was the right decision. "I don't want to take a chance on losing Koko again. And there's not much back there for us, either. What do you say, Koko? Want to stay here with Wayne and Sammie?"

Koko looked up at Erik. She tilted her head and smiled.

Then she ran into the maze.

"Koko, no!" Erik shouted, but she didn't stop. He watched her run down the entrance row, then lost her when she turned right at the first intersection.

Erik froze. His eyes darted from the maze to Wayne and back again. Wayne patted him on the shoulder. "Go," he said. "Your dog needs you."

Erik ran into the maze after her. At the first intersection, he stopped and looked back at Wayne and Sammie, standing together in the parking lot. Wayne waved good-bye, while Sammie barked and lifted her paw. Erik nodded, then turned right and went after Koko.

At the next intersection, night descended, as sudden as if someone had flipped a switch. One second it was daylight, with bright blue skies overhead, the next it was dark. Millions of stars twinkled above him, even more than he'd seen on the shores of that ancient sea. One moon hung low on the horizon to his right; the second hung low to his left. It felt as though he were looking into the furnace of creation. He stood there, mesmerized. The urge to sit down and lose himself was hard to resist. He may have done it, too, except Koko's bark snapped him back to reality.

Her next bark came from one row over. "Stay there, girl, I'm coming!" Erik crashed through the row and emerged onto another path. Koko wasn't there.

She barked again, farther away to his right this time. He turned to orient himself. A few seconds later, her bark came from far behind him.

"Koko, stop!" he yelled. How was she moving so fast? There was no way she could get from one side of the maze to the other that quickly. He had to find her. They couldn't have come all this way just to lose each other again.

*Woof!*

Erik jumped. Koko was right next to him. Except she wasn't. He could hear the jingle of her collar, her happy panting, but he couldn't see her. He fell to the ground, feeling around for her. He felt a lick on his face, smelled her breath, then a brush of her fur along his calf, and then nothing.

Koko was gone.

# CHAPTER TWENTY-NINE

"Think we'll see them again, Sammie?" She shook her head. "Yeah, me neither." Wayne picked up his pack and slung it over his shoulder. He'd come back for the rest of their gear later. "Let's go check out the farmhouse. Maybe we'll stay here for a few days, just in case they come back."

Sammie trotted ahead and jumped up on the porch. "Whoa, wait a minute." Wayne's laugh was bittersweet. "I need you to catch some dinner first."

Sammie barked and hopped back off the porch. "And stay out of the maze!"

He sat on the steps and leaned his crutch against the railing, then watched Sammie run into the woods across the road. Was that part of the Eris Ridge Trail? In Shelly's world, it was a few miles from the maze. But this wasn't Shelly's world. Did it matter in the end? *Not really*, he decided.

He heard Sammie bark, happy to be on the hunt again. It wasn't long before she'd caught three squixels, along with another creature he'd never seen before. It looked like a cross between a rabbit and a small fox, or maybe a racoon. "What do you bet it tastes like chicken?" he asked as he skinned the animals.

After dinner, he and Sammie settled next to the fire. He smiled as he listened to the peepers and the crickets. Somewhere in the woods, a whippoorwill cried out. "You're a little late," he told it. "I'm the only one left."

Sensing the sadness in his voice, Sammie nuzzled his hand.

He didn't know what to make of the area above the maze. The stars, even the darkness itself, didn't match the surrounding sky, as if another reality were pushing its way through. At one point, he swore he could see a satellite passing through the firmament. *Are there people somewhere still controlling it,* he wondered, *or is it broadcasting data back to a dead world?*

The sound of something sneaking along the far side of the farmhouse interrupted his reverie. "Did you hear that, Sammie?" She lifted her head, sniffed the air, and went back to sleep. "Guess I must have imagined it." He willfully ignored the fact that dangerous creatures had crept up on them before without the dogs noticing. There was nothing he could do about it anyway, not with his bum ankle.

"What do you say we call it a night, girl?" He lifted himself up with his crutch, then threw some dirt on the fire. His canteen was almost empty, so he didn't want to waste the little water he had left. With any luck, the place had a well somewhere, or they'd find a creek or a pond nearby. He'd worry about it in the morning.

Once they were inside the farmhouse, he decided he wasn't up to climbing the stairs, which meant he'd be sleeping on the living room sofa. A thick cloud of dust exploded when he smacked the cushions, but at least there was nothing living in them. He lay down and was asleep within minutes.

When he woke up, sunlight was streaming through the front windows. Sammie was gone. *Must have needed to pee*, he thought. *Me too*. There wasn't a bathroom on the first floor, and he still didn't feel up to climbing the stairs, so he walked out onto the porch, thinking he'd just hop out to the edge of the maze and pee there.

He froze. There were footprints in the dirt around the porch, around the firepit, and on the steps. He put his boot next to one of them. It was a different size.

In all, he found five sets of strange footprints around the house. None of them were his.

Were they friendly? Should he be worried? The fact that they hadn't killed him in his sleep gave him hope.

And where the heck was Sammie?

He hopped back up onto the porch and sat in the rocker. She'd show up, eventually.

Sammie's barking woke him. He must have dozed off. He grabbed his crutch and pushed himself out of the chair. "Sammie, where are you? Get back here!"

She didn't come back.

He gripped his knife and limped down the steps.

A man walked around from the side of the house. Wayne raised his knife; the man raised his hands. "Whoa, no need for that," he said. "We're friendly."

"We? How many are you? And where's my dog?" Wayne raised the knife higher.

"She's right here," a woman answered. She walked out with Sammie by her side.

Wayne took a step back. His hands fell to his side, and he dropped the knife. It was Lori, his wife. His *dead* wife.

"Lori...?" Wayne's voice trembled. "Is it really you?

How...? You died in the accident. Oh my god, I've missed you so much."

The woman smiled. "I'm sorry, but I don't think we've met." She petted Sammie. "My name isn't Lori. It's Heather. What's yours?"

Wayne choked back a sob. "It's *me*, Wayne. Your husband. Don't you recognize me? Or Sammie?" His mind couldn't accept that this woman wasn't his wife.

Heather shook her head. "I've never been married." She held up her left hand and wiggled her fingers. "Still happily single. But if you say I look like your wife, I believe you. Anything's possible over here. Isn't that right, Sammie?" Sammie jumped up and hugged her. "I think she likes me."

Wayne didn't say anything. He couldn't.

The man's eyes widened. "Wait, you're Wayne?" He took a closer look at Sammie. "Of course. Wayne and Sammie! Sammie and Wayne! It all makes sense now."

A wave of dizziness swept over Wayne. He limped back over to the porch and sat down, worried he might pass out. "What do you mean it all makes sense now? Nothing makes sense about any of this."

"I can see where you might be a little confused," the man said. "So, let's start with the basics. My name is Jordon. You've met Heather."

Heather waved, then went back to petting Sammie.

"This doppelganger thing between you two is new." Jordon pointed at Wayne, then Heather. "We should definitely talk more about it later."

"No shit," Wayne snorted.

"And I apologize for not recognizing you and Sammie sooner. I should have put two and two together and led with that. That's on me." He bowed his head. "As to how I know your names, that's an interesting story. A while back,

I'd say several months, maybe a year, who knows the way time moves here, I mean, it could've been more than a year—"

"Jordon, focus," Heather said. "Let's just say a year."

Jordon bowed again. "Right, right, let's say a year ago, we ran into a young couple wandering on their own—"

Wayne practically jumped out of his seat. Sammie came over and stood next to him. "Craig and Shelly? They're alive?"

"Bingo." Jordon grinned. "Craig and Shelly."

"But... How? They disappeared when they killed the beast. We didn't know if they were dead or alive or what."

"Well, I don't know if they killed that thing or not," Jordon said. "If it even *can* be killed, for that matter. But, yes, Craig and Shelly are definitely still alive. At least they were the last time we saw them."

Wayne couldn't believe it. *Craig and Shelly are alive!* "So what happened? Are they okay? Where are they?" He swung his head around, looking for them.

Jordon held up his hands. "Whoa, cowboy. One question at a time."

Wayne nodded and sat back down.

Jordon held up his index finger. "Question the first," he said. "They don't know what happened. Shelly said they thought they were going to die. The last thing she remembered was a bright white flash, and then they woke up in a field. There was no sign of the beast." Jordon held up his middle finger. "Question the second: they're fine. Better than fine, actually. Just a couple happy little lovebirds, those two. Right, Heather?"

Heather smiled. "They make a cute couple. They were worried about you and Sammie, though. Erik and Koko, too." She swept her gaze across the yard. "Are they around here somewhere? We saw you and Sammie by the fire last night, but nobody else."

Wayne shook his head. "No, I don't know where they are, either. Koko ran into the corn maze right after we lost Craig and Shelly, and Erik followed her. That was the last I saw of them."

"I'm not surprised," Jordon said. "People who go in there don't come back out."

"Do you know what happens to them?"

"No idea. We've heard stories, of course, but who knows if they're true or not. Nobody in our group ever wanted to test them out. We like it here."

"I get that," Wayne said. "Sammie and I are happy here, too."

"I don't think Craig and Shelly are," Heather said. "They're happy to have found each other, but they want to go home."

"Which brings us to question the third." Jordon held up his ring finger. "They stayed with us for a week or so, then took off. As far as we know, they're still out there looking for a way back."

"I hope they find it," Heather said.

"We all do," Jordon said.

"We *all*...?" Wayne asked. "How many more are in your group? I counted five sets of footprints this morning."

Jordon clicked his tongue. "Nothing gets by you, does it?" He tilted his head toward the road. "The others are in the woods, waiting. We didn't want to overwhelm you. In all, there are twelve, including me and Heather. That makes you unlucky number thirteen."

Wayne frowned.

"I'm sorry, just a little numerology joke," Jordon said.

"You're thirteen, but Sammie's number fourteen, so we're good, right Sammie?"

Sammie barked in agreement.

Wayne raised his hand. "Hold up. You said you ran into Craig and Shelly a year ago, right?"

"Well, Heather said it was a year ago. I said it *could* have been a year ago. It could also have been several months. Or maybe more than a year."

"Fine, fine, fine," Wayne said, holding his palm up. "Here's the thing. Craig and Shelly just disappeared *yesterday*."

Jordon leaned forward and furrowed his eyebrows. "Interesting. We should talk more about that later, too."

"Let me ask you about Sammie," Heather said, changing the subject. "Have you noticed anything different about her since coming over?"

"Oh yeah. She's smarter and younger compared to how she was back home."

"Our dog Frankie is really smart, too. Like super-smart. But what do you mean by younger?" Heather asked.

"Sammie's an old girl, and her arthritis was pretty bad. She'd get a little confused sometimes, too. Nothing anyone but me would notice, but still..." Wayne rubbed Sammie's head. "Over here, though? All that's gone. It's like she's five or six years old again."

"That's interesting," Heather said. "Frankie seems young, but we don't know how old he was when he came over."

"Speaking of, where are you from?" Jordon asked. "And when?"

"Idaho Springs, Colorado," Wayne said. "2020."

"2020, huh? You're our first from that year."

"What about you?" Wayne asked.

"Sedona, Arizona. 2027. I always thought all those stories about vortexes was just a bunch of hokum to bring in the almighty tourism dollars," Jordon said. He raised his hands and shrugged. "Oops."

Wayne chuckled. "Oops is right. What about you, Heather?"

"West Indiana, 1983."

"Not *western* Indiana, mind you," Jordon interjected. "But the actual state of West Indiana. It's one of fifty-seven states."

"Fifty-eight, actually," Heather corrected him.

Wayne's jaw dropped.

Jordon grinned. "Oh, it gets weirder, my friend. We also have a pioneer woman from 1892. And a couple kids from the '30s. Plus an older man who we think might be Russian."

"You don't happen to speak Russian, do you?" Heather asked. "Or any Eastern European language?"

Wayne shook his head. "Sorry, high school Spanish is as far as I got."

"That's too bad. We're pretty good at communicating through gestures, but I'd love to know his story."

Nearby, a dog barked. Sammie's ears perked up, and she ran out to meet a small yellow dog as it trotted out from the woods.

"There's Frankie," said Jordon. "We don't know how he got here, but his rabies tag is from San Antonio, 1967."

Wayne took a moment to collect his thoughts, then gave up. "I don't know what to say."

"That's okay. It's a lot to take in," Heather said. "But don't worry. You can take all the time you need. It's the one thing we have plenty of."

# CHAPTER THIRTY

"*Koko! Koko! Where are you?*" Erik didn't know how long he'd been searching for her in the maze, but it felt like hours. His voice was almost gone. He was tired. Hungry. Thirsty. Tassels tangled in his hair and stuck to his sweaty skin. The leaves had cut his arms and legs. He'd walked through, around, and behind the rows looking for her. The maze seemed to have no end. The alien night sky still shone overhead, the moons drifting in circles along the periphery.

When he couldn't go any farther, he collapsed.

He woke to the sound of voices from nearby. *People!* Excited, he ran toward the source of the voices, but they were constantly moving. Up one row and down another he ran, crashing through rows when the voices didn't get any closer. Finally, he burst through one row and stumbled out into the parking lot. He had to shield his eyes against the blinding midday sun.

"Hey, you! What are you doing in my maze?" An old man came running across the lot toward him, shaking his fist. Erik took a couple of steps back. A wave of dizziness washed over him, and he passed out.

When he came to, he was lying on a couch. The old man was sitting next to him, wringing out a washcloth, which he pressed against Erik's forehead. Erik tried to sit up, but the man gently pushed him back down.

"Where am I?" asked Erik. "Who are you? Where's Koko?"

"Whoa, whoa, slow down, son," the old man said. "One question at a time. One, you're in my farmhouse. Two, I'm Bob, although most people call me Old Bob. Three, I don't know who Koko is. You're the only person who came out of the maze."

Erik pushed himself to a sitting position. "*You're* Old Bob? Of Old Bob's Corn Maize Spooktacular?"

"You've heard of me!" Old Bob bowed his head. "The one and only."

"Man, am I happy to see you."

"And I'm happy to see you, too." His face turned serious. "And now I'd like to know how you got into my maze."

"Through the front entrance," Erik said.

"No, you didn't. You weren't in there last night when we did a sweep. You weren't in there during our morning sweep, either. And we didn't see you on any of the cameras."

Erik cocked his head. "You have cameras?"

"Yeah, we have the whole place under surveillance," Old Bob said. "For instances just like this. You're what we call a visitor."

"A *visitor*." Something clicked in Erik's head. "That's right, Shelly told me about your visitors."

Now it was Old Bob's turn to look surprised. "Shelly

Perkins, that reporter from the *Chronicle*? Nobody's seen her since she went missing three years ago."

"Yeah, on the night she interviewed you," Erik said. It was all coming back to him now. "You told her about a shortcut on the Eris Ridge Trail. She took it and disappeared from the face of the earth."

"How do you know all that?" Old Bob's eyes narrowed.

"Shelly told me," Erik said.

Old Bob's head jerked back in shock. "You've talked to her? How is she? *Where* is she? Her family went crazy after she vanished. Her father actually moved up here. Rented a house in town. Spent the next nine months looking for her. I swear he knew the back roads as well as I did by the time he left. Finally gave up and returned home when his wife threatened to leave him. I don't think he'd given up hope, but she'd had enough."

"I talked to her yesterday," Erik said. "But I don't know where she is now." He dropped his voice. "Or when, for that matter."

"*When*? What does that even mean?"

"It's a long story," Erik sighed. "I don't think you'd believe it."

Old Bob chuckled. "Son, you'd be surprised by what I believe these days."

Erik thought for a moment. "Yeah, maybe you would. But first, I need to get to the Eris Ridge Trail. Shelly said it's just a few miles from here. Can you give me directions?"

Old Bob didn't want to; he wanted Erik to stay and talk to the sheriff. But Erik wouldn't take no for an answer. Eventually, Old Bob relented and drew him a map. "Are you sure you don't want me to drive you?"

"Thanks, but I'd rather walk. It'll help clear my head."

"Are you coming back?"

Erik thought about it. With any luck, he wouldn't. But he didn't want to disappoint Old Bob, so he told him he would if he could.

"Can I tell Shelly's dad I talked to you?"

"Please do. Tell him his daughter meant a lot to me. She saved my life on more than one occasion. And the lives of my friends."

Old Bob insisted Erik take some food and water with him. He made him a couple of sandwiches and filled a canteen. Erik stuck out his hand, but Old Bob pulled him in for a hug. "I hope you find what you're looking for," he said, then walked him to the parking lot. When Erik reached the end of the driveway, Old Bob yelled after him. "Hey, you never told me who Koko was!"

"Black Border Collie, jingly red collar. And the best dog in the whole world. If you see her, tell her I'm looking for her."

"You want me to tell a dog you're looking for her?"

"She'll understand," Erik said. He waved goodbye and headed down the road.

It took about an hour before he saw the sign for the Eris Ridge Trail, and another ten minutes before he reached it. It was just as Shelly had described.

He pulled out the canteen and took a sip. The sun was low on the horizon. He guessed it would be full dark in an hour or so. That was good. About three miles down the trail, Erik heard an approaching car. He moved to the side of the trail and kept walking, leaving plenty of room for it to drive by.

A minute later, the car pulled up next to him. The driver, an attractive woman—in her early thirties, he guessed—slowed down and lowered the window. "Need a ride?"

Erik smiled. "No thanks, I'm good."

"Are you sure? It'll be dark soon. You don't want to be on the trail after the sun goes down. Not by yourself, at least."

"Oh yeah? Why's that?" Erik was curious to hear what she had to say.

"Weird things happen. Strange animal sightings. Lights in the sky. A few years ago, a reporter disappeared near here. On a night a lot like this one, actually."

"Yeah, I heard about her," Erik said. "Pretty spooky stuff." He started walking again.

The car crept alongside him, keeping pace. "Are you sure you don't want a ride?"

Erik was about to say no again when a black puppy poked its head up from the passenger seat and yipped at him.

"Careful, puppy," the woman said, laughing. "Don't jump out. I don't want you to get lost again."

Erik walked up to the car. The woman put it in park. "What's your dog's name?" he asked. "And what do you mean lost again?"

"I don't know." The woman scratched the puppy's head as she talked. "I found her wandering down the road not long before I turned onto the trail. No idea who she belongs to. No collar or tags. She's obviously lost, though. Old Bob's is the only place around here for miles, and I know she doesn't belong to him. The trail here's a shortcut to town. I wouldn't normally take it this late in the day, but I wanted to get there before the vet closes. Maybe he'll know her owner."

Erik couldn't answer her as he was being smothered in puppy kisses. The puppy looked exactly like Koko had when he'd picked her out at the shelter eighteen years ago. It wasn't possible. *Couldn't* be possible. But he knew it was her.

"You know what, I think I will take that ride," he said. "If the offer still stands."

"Well, the puppy sure seems to like you, so that's good enough for me. Hop in."

Erik sat down and closed the door. He fastened his seat belt and leaned the seat back a bit. The puppy stretched out across his chest and went to sleep.

"I'm Samantha," the woman said. "My friends call me Sam."

"Erik." He closed his eyes. "Thanks for the ride, Sam. I'm glad you stopped."

"Where you headed, Erik?"

"Surprise me."

# ACKNOWLEDGMENTS

Oy, a second book. Who would've thunk it, right? Certainly not me. Especially if you'd've told me it'd be a 36,000-word novella, when I'd never written anything longer than a 5,700-word short story up to this point.

But there were things in four stories in my collection *The Space Between*—the title story, "Strange Constellations," "The Tunnel at the End of the Light," and "Lost at Last"—that I just couldn't get out of my head. Settings that needed to be explored. Characters who wouldn't shut up. Endings that ended too soon.

So I picked up pen and paper (actually pen and tablet, as these days I write my first drafts longhand on my Galaxy Tab) and got to work. Not gonna lie, it was intimidating as hell, and there were more than a few times I almost chucked the whole thing. But I'm glad I didn't.

I hope you are, too.

You don't need to have read any of the stories in my collection to follow this one. It's a completely standalone piece. But it will give you deeper insight into the characters. Of course, because I'm a total doofus, I had to change the name of the MC in "The Space Between" from Erik to Craig, because otherwise I'd have two characters named Erik in this one.

Funny story about that name. I use Erik as a placeholder name in most of my first drafts until a better name comes to me. And that's because I was supposed to be an

Erik. In fact, my name was supposed to be Erik Vaughn Hinkle, which sounds like some badass European aristocracy. Can you imagine the first impressions I could've made with a name like that? Instead, my parents just stuck a Jr. on the end of my dad's name and called it a day.

Speaking of parents, I wish they were around to see this. Especially my mom, Barbara, who was my original Constant Reader. I wish Sammie and Koko were here for it, too.

People I need to thank who *are* still around (at least at the time of this writing) include the Monday Night Write Club (Terry Emery, Ken Godfrey, Valerie Williams, and Mary Anne Back), who dutifully read my shitty first drafts of every chapter, beta reader Cory Cone, and MNWC partners in crime Tom Deady and Christa Carmen, who held my hand every step of the way, often at the same time as they were kicking my ass to keep going.

My editor Linda Nagle was an invaluable resource, helping to smooth down the rough edges and fix my sloppy grammar and abundant typos. (If you find any typos, they're my fault, not hers. I'm a constant tinkerer and probably screwed something up after she handed it back to me.)

A huge shout-out to my cover artist, François Vaillancourt. It's like he reached inside my head and pulled out exactly what I wanted my cover to look like, except it's even better than I could've imagined.

And final thanks go to my wife Vanessa, who puts up with my nonsense while giving me the space and support I need to bring these stories to life. Without her, there'd be no Eris Ridge Trail.

Larry Hinkle, 1-19-2025

# ABOUT THE AUTHOR

Larry Hinkle is the least famous writer you've never heard of. A copywriter living with his wife and two doggos in Rockville, Maryland, when he's not writing stories that scare people into peeing their pants, he writes ads that scare people into buying adult diapers, so they're not caught peeing their pants.

His debut collection, *The Space Between*, was published in February 2024 by Trepidatio Publishing. Additionally, his work has appeared in *The Rack: Stories Inspired by Vintage Horror Paperbacks*; *October Screams: A Halloween Anthology*; and The NoSleep Podcast, among others.

He's an active member of the HWA (his short stories made the preliminary Stoker ballot in 2020 and 2022); a graduate of Fright Club and Crystal Lake's Author's Journey short story and novella programs; an HWA mentee; and a survivor of the Borderlands Writers Bootcamp.

Stop by and visit him at thatscarylarry.com or stalk him on the socials at @thatscarylarry.